CHASING DEMONS

CHASING DEMONS

Christy Tillery French

Mystery and Suspense Press
New York Lincoln Shanghai

Chasing Demons

Mystery and Suspense Press
an imprint of iUniverse, Inc.

For information address:
iUniverse, Inc.
2021 Pine Lake Road, Suite 100
Lincoln, NE 68512
www.iuniverse.com

ISBN: 0-595-29123-6

Printed in the United States of America

For my parents: Margie Clark, a woman of remarkable inner strength and beauty, whose love for the written word engendered in me a love for writing; and John Tillery, unsurpassable artist and storyteller, who introduced me to the wondrous beauty of the Black Mountains of North Carolina. With love.

"For what is evil but good tortured by its own hunger and thirst?"

—Kahlil Gibran
The Prophet

Acknowledgements

The author wishes to thank the following people: Lt. Cynthia Gass with the Knoxville Police Department for discussing with me the rules of protocol concerning hostage negotiation; former policeman turned author David Hunter for his sage advice and for answering my questions regarding police procedure and bullets; Duke Gard, who not only explained but showed to me the vast differences in handguns; John McElroy for his input regarding loading weapons; authors Victoria Taylor Murray, Sherry Russell, Laurel Johnson, and Lynn Barry, my dear friends and colleagues who keep me buoyed and moving forward; author Evelyn Horan for not only being a friend but teacher, as well; my sister Cyndi Hodges for continuing to share the dream with me and creating one of her own which I can now share with her; and last but not least, my beautiful family Steve, Jon, and Meghann for making my world so much brighter.

CHAPTER 1

▼

The woman's eyes were wide with horror, disbelief. She looked into his own, pleading with him to not let this man hurt her, not let her die, not like this, to not leave her. All without saying a word, all with only her eyes, which were beautiful: large, dark-gray ovals framed with thick, ebony lashes. Eyes that would never leave him for the rest of his life. He reached out to her, was within inches of pulling her from harm, when his face was spattered with pieces of her flesh, tissue, brain; drenched with hot blood. Feeling all this before hearing the fatal shot.

Garth awakened with a start, seeing those eyes dying, the light fading; catching at that final moment the accusation in the woman's eyes as she looked into his. Knowing the last thought she had on earth was that this man had let her down, had not saved her as she had so desperately needed, wanted him to do.

Garth groaned, forced himself to sit up, and waited for the shaking to subside. He wiped the sweat from his brow as he willed the images away. Rising, he glanced out the window, noticed darkness had descended, and cursed himself for thinking once again that maybe he would be lucky this time and he would not see those eyes when his own were closed in sleep.

At the kitchen door, Garth paused, swaying slightly, still sweating. He barely registered the softly whining dog nudging at his hand with its nose. He yanked his jacket off the coat-rack, threw the door open, and stomped to the stables, murmuring, "I'm sorry, I'm so sorry," never realizing these words were his mantra each time he awakened.

Close to the barn, the dog stopped, raised his nose, sniffed, and began to throw his head this way and that as he trotted ahead.

Entering the stables, Garth instinctively felt that something was amiss but dismissed it as his reaction to the dog's behavior. He began to check the stalls one by one, ascertaining the horses had entered on their own and were patiently awaiting the corn and rolled-oats combination he fed them each evening.

The dog had gone to the farthest stall and was now emitting bursts of frustrated whines, darting looks inside the enclosure and then back to Garth, as if to urge him to come see.

Garth ignored the animal, thinking one of the cats or maybe a field mouse or rat had caught his attention. He murmured soothing words to the horses, stroking muzzles reaching out to him. He closed the lower halves of the stall doors as he moved toward the one at the end occupied by his favored horse.

Garth became alarmed when he didn't see the Tennessee Walker waiting on him, which was unusual. Peering further into the stall, he grew puzzled at the sight of the young horse reclining on his side in the far corner. Garth had never known him to lie down at mealtime.

The dog darted toward the large animal, then away, emitting short barks, as if to say, hurry up, why don't you. He would not go too close to the horse, having a healthy respect for the damage his hooves could inflict.

Garth shooed the dog away so that he wouldn't be hurt if the gelding got feisty. "Anything wrong, boy?" he asked, entering the stall, wondering if the animal had gotten tangled in barbwire again. The horse raised his head and snickered at him but did not rise.

Garth approached carefully, aware of the strength of this animal, knowing he could be killed from one kick, knowing if the horse was in pain, he would strike out at anyone or anything.

Garth murmured reassuringly as he knelt close to the horse's head. He stroked the gelding as he looked him over. His eyes stopped at what lay behind.

Something wrapped in a horse blanket was bundled up against the back of the stall. Garth could see tufts of dark hair but nothing else. He reached out, drew the blanket back, and felt his body jolt at the sight of those same eyes he had just witnessed in his dream. "Jesus," he grunted, shifting his weight, losing his balance, and landing on his rear.

The dog, which had been peering over Garth's shoulder, leapt back, yelping in alarm.

Garth closed his eyes and tried to gather his wits, telling himself he hadn't actually seen what he had just dreamt. "It's okay, Boo," he said to the dog, more as a means of reassuring himself than anything else. He forced himself to move toward the blanket once more, forced himself to look at the face more closely. He was thankful the eyes were now closed and realized with relief this was not the same face that had housed the eyes that dwelt in his dreams. He slowly drew the blanket away and felt his heart lurch when the eyes came open suddenly, widely, looking at him with the same alarm as in his dream.

The woman reached toward him, and he instinctively moved back away from her. Boo let out a bark of alarm. "Don't let him find me," the woman pleaded with him in a weak voice. "He killed my baby. Please don't let him find me, he'll…" She closed those eyes again and her body went slack.

Garth reached out and shook her slightly. "Miss?" he asked her, then, "Miss?" When she didn't respond to him, he stood, urged the horse up with him, and moved him to the far side of the stall. He bent down, picked the woman up in his arms, and carried her to the house. The dog trailed behind, sniffing the air.

Garth took the unconscious woman to the extra bedroom and lay her on the day bed, unsure what to do with her. He noticed his arms and stomach felt wet and turned on the lamp by the bed. His eyes widened at the dark red splotches, then darted to the bloodstained blanket.

"My God," he said in a raspy voice, as he gently peeled the blanket away. His eyes traveled the woman's body, taking in the dark stains on her lower sweater and jeans. He straightened up, walked to the window, and stood there, staring at her, wondering what in the hell had happened. Boo sat watching him, every once in awhile issuing a worried whine.

Garth finally pulled a quilt from the closet and covered her. He walked out of the room, to the kitchen, and called the only close friend he had: Thad Brownlee, a nurse practitioner who also served as their small community's veterinarian, although he did not have the license to go with it.

"Thad," Garth said into the phone. "It's Garth. I need your help. It's—well, I guess it's an emergency. Can you come now?"

He listened for a second. "I'll leave the door unlocked, just come on in." Ignoring Thad's queries as to which animal was in jeopardy, he hung up the phone and returned to the bedroom.

Garth had had medical training as a policeman but didn't want to do any more damage than had been done. After ascertaining there wasn't a steady flow of blood that he could detect, he waited for Thad. He paced back and forth as he watched the woman beneath the quilt, the dog keeping pace with him.

When his friend entered the house, Garth left the room to meet him. He told him as he led him to the bedroom what he had found in the barn and about the blood. "Jesus, Thad, there's so much blood, I don't see how she could still be alive."

Thad uncovered the woman, then glanced at Garth. "Why didn't you call 911 or take her to the hospital?" he asked as he removed the now-bloody quilt and dropped it on the floor.

"Before she passed out, she said something about not letting someone find her, that he'd killed her baby, he'd kill her, I think. I could barely understand her," Garth said, watching his friend.

Thad ceased his visual examination and approached Garth. "If someone's after her and they did this to her, then they sure as hell aren't going to stop because of you. Come on, let's take her to the hospital."

Garth remained silent, watching the woman.

"I'm not a doctor, Gar. I can't help her, not like they can. Come on, let's get her in the car."

"Wait a minute." Garth continued to stare at the unconscious woman. "She looks familiar, Thad. I think I know her." He approached the bed, stooped down, and gently pushed her hair away from her face. He leaned close to her, studying her features. "Damn," he said in a low voice.

Thad joined him. "What?"

Garth glanced at him. "You know who this is?"

Thad peered down at the woman's pale, upturned face. "No, I don't think so." He leaned down to regard her more closely.

"Angel Salvatori, wife of Tony Salvatori," Garth muttered.

"Who?"

"Biggest kingpin in the Southeast." Garth's eyes returned to the woman. "Connected to the mob; controls all the drugs, firearms, prostitution, gambling, anything illegal you could think of. KPD Vice has been after that guy hot and heavy as long as he's been in Knoxville."

Thad's face held a worried expression. "Uh-oh."

"There are bodies all over East Tennessee because of him." Garth glanced at his friend. "He's a violent, dangerous man. If she's running from him for some reason, then she wasn't lying when she said he'd kill her. People have been known to die just for looking at the man the wrong way."

Thad's face blanched. "Are you sure it's her? I mean, it may be someone that looks like her, you know."

Garth shook his head. "No, it's her. I actually met her a couple of times when I lived in Knoxville."

"Oh, man," Thad said in a low voice.

"Can you help her?"

Thad thought a moment. "You got any scissors?"

Garth cocked his head at him.

"We'll probably need to cut these clothes off her, find out where all this blood is coming from."

As Thad cut, then removed the clothes, Garth peeled them away, both men uttering curses at the ugly discoloration covering the woman's upper stomach, back, and arms. When they removed her pants, Garth stood at the sight of her abdomen and thighs, which were covered with bruises and contusions. Her panties were soaked with blood.

They looked at one another.

"You think she's been raped?" Garth asked.

Thad began to cut her underwear away. "I don't know. Go get a bucket of very warm water and some antibacterial soap."

When Garth returned, Thad had covered his patient with a sheet. He stood to take the bucket from Garth. "She's had a miscarriage, looks like. That's where most of the blood's from. We need to clean her up, though, make sure it isn't anything more than that."

While Thad cleaned the lower part of her body, Garth drew another bucket of warm water. He washed her face and upper torso, feeling embarrassed at tending to an unconscious, naked woman.

After Thad finished, he glanced at Garth. "I don't suppose you have any sanitary pads here, do you? Or panties, for that matter."

Garth took the time to frown at him. "I'm a bachelor. Why would I have those things?"

Thad grinned slightly. "You were married at one time, you know," he reminded his friend.

"Yeah and when she left, not only did she take everything that belonged to her, she took everything that belonged to me."

A smile skittered across Thad's lips. "I don't know, I thought maybe there'd been a girlfriend in the woodwork sometime since then."

"I have no interest in letting another woman into my life," Garth said in a terse manner, causing Thad to wonder about this.

"You're going to have to go into town and get them, then."

"You mean, the pads and the—the…"

Thad smiled.

Garth gave him an irritated scowl. "And how do you expect me to explain why I'm making those purchases?"

"Hey, your business is your business," Thad replied equably. "Who said you have to explain anything to anybody? But she'll probably bleed for a few days and she needs those things."

Garth thought for a moment, then finally said, in a grudging tone, "Where exactly would I go to get them?"

Thad looked askance at him. "You mean to tell me, you were married, what, three years and you never once purchased either of those items for your wife?"

Garth's brow furrowed.

"Oh, I forgot. You're the big, bad policeman. Guys like you don't do things like that."

Garth visibly bristled but held his tongue.

Thad thought. "Wal-Mart, I guess, or KMart. Any drugstore."

"You'll stay here with her till I get back?"

Thad nodded, then turned his attention back to the woman, who was moaning lowly.

Garth walked toward his bedroom, shucking his shirt as he went. He threw the stained clothing into the bathroom hamper, then washed the blood off his hands. In his bedroom, he pulled a flannel shirt out of the closet and buttoned it as he headed back to the guest room. He stood in the doorway, digging his truck keys out of his pants pocket. "You think she's going to be okay?"

"I hope so." Thad said distractedly as he lifted the sheet, checking for blood.

"I'll be right back," Garth said, feeling uncomfortable watching his friend.

Thad added as Garth left, "You might want to pick up some ibuprofen or Extra-Strength Tylenol. She's not going to be feeling too good when she wakes up. Plus she'll have cramps from the miscarriage."

"Maybe I should have taken her to the hospital," Garth muttered.

CHAPTER 2

▼

Garth drove to the nearest store, which was a combination convenience store and self-help gas station located on the outskirts of the picturesque town of Black Mountain, North Carolina. He entered, hoping no one he knew would be in there this late at night. He checked around, found the pads and ibuprofen, but no panties. "Shoulda known," he said to himself and drove to Wal-Mart, which was further away.

Garth strolled into the department store, thankful there weren't many people frequenting it this late at night, and ambled around, trying to appear as if he were browsing. He found the health-and-beauty section and walked down the aisles until he located the sanitary napkins. He studied them, wondering which ones he should get. There were all kinds, confusing him. Should he buy the ones with wings or without? And what the hell were wings anyway? Overnight or daytime use? Long or regular length? Mini, mini-maxi, maxi or maxi-maxi? Contoured or flat? "Oh, hell," he grumbled, reached out and grabbed a package off the shelf. In the pharmacy department, he picked out Wal-Mart's brand of ibuprofen, then headed toward the women's section.

Garth had a major dilemma there, not knowing what size underwear the woman wore. Shoot, even when he was married, he never bought lingerie for his wife, never even had the slightest inclination to, letting her handle that. He studied the multitude of panties hanging up, then noticed the ones that were packaged. He recognized the Hanes brand name and regarded the selection with some confusion. He became aware of a woman who looked to be in her early twenties warily watching him. Garth ignored her, finally deciding if he got a medium, surely that would fit. Large would be too big, he was certain of that, but would she be considered a small woman? She looked small to him, but then, so had his wife, although he did remember seeing the M tag on several of her clothes.

He noticed the young woman staring and shrugged his shoulders. "Not sure of the size."

She drew closer. "You know what size pants she wears?"

Garth shook his head.

"Well, unless she's real tiny, I guess a medium size would be the best choice, then," she said, voicing what Garth had been considering. She looked at him. "Unless she's kind of, you know," she hesitated, then said, "big," holding her hands out to either side.

"I would definitely not categorize her as a big woman," Garth said.

The young woman wandered over and stood beside him, considering the sundry selection. She turned to him. "You think she might be about my size?"

Garth stepped back and gave her a quick study, then a pained look. "To tell you the truth, I don't hardly know the wom—I mean, I just met her and never really looked at her to detect her, um, size, so I don't—well, maybe she is. I don't know."

She gave him a look.

"What?" he asked, unsettled by this.

"You're buying panties for a woman you just met, a woman you don't know what size she is?" she asked with disbelief. "You can't even guess what size she is? I mean, have you even seen this woman?" Her eyes widened. "Ohhhh." She gave him a different look, one he didn't like in the least.

"What?"

"If I were you, I'd get a large size. As tall as you are, that should work."

He got it now. "Hey, these aren't for me," he said, in a raised voice.

Two older women who were browsing nearby turned and stared at him.

Garth glanced at them, then back to the young woman. "Thanks for your help. I think I can manage."

"Sure thing, pervert." She moved away from him, giving him a suspicious look.

Garth turned back to the panties. Okay, medium. But wait a minute. They were sized by number. He looked for a chart showing which numbers went with which sizes but couldn't find any. He studied the range of numbers, trying to gauge which ones the medium would fall into, and finally decided a five ought to be close enough. Anyway, it would have to do.

Now another dilemma presented itself. Did she wear high-rise, bikini-cut, sports-cut, full-cut, thongs? Well, he sure as hell wasn't going to buy the woman thongs. Why couldn't women's underwear be like men's, he wondered with great irritation. You had two simple choices: jockeys or boxers. Why make something that should be so easy so difficult? He caught movement out of the corner of his eye and glanced that way. The young woman had now teamed up with the two older women and all were looking his way and whispering furiously. Realizing he was drawing attention he definitely did not want nor need, a red-faced Garth reached out and grabbed a package of six, multicolored, cotton panties.

Garth found a register without a line and placed his purchases down, thankful he had gotten by without being recognized. He pulled out his wallet, hoping he wouldn't run into the young lady who called him a pervert.

"Mr. Fisher?" a voice asked from behind, startling him.

A woman he vaguely recalled meeting at some function or other was smiling at him. Garth gave her a quick smile in return. "How are you?" he asked politely, trying vainly to remember her name, which seemed out of reach.

"I'm just fine, I reckon." Her voice had a raspy quality, signaling to Garth she was an avid smoker. "Haven't seen you around town much lately."

"I stay pretty busy," Garth said, his tone noncommittal.

The woman's eyes strayed to the items the register operator was pulling toward her to scan. Her eyebrows went up. "I thought you were single."

Garth felt his face go red.

"Oh, of course, these must be for your girlfriend," she nosily inquired.

Garth desperately tried to think of an excuse for the purchases. He didn't want anyone to even suspect he had a woman at his cabin, especially Tony Salvatori's runaway bride. "Uh, no. Actually, they're for my animals," he finally sputtered.

She gave him an uncertain smile. "Your animals?"

He gave her a weak smile as he searched his mind for a realistic purpose for the items. "Well, the, uh, the pads make great bandages for horses. They're large enough to—well, my gelding seems to like getting tangled up in barbwire, and it's easier using one of those, uh, things as a bandage instead of gauze. They're thicker, they stay put better."

She seemed to be enjoying this. "And the underpants? Surely they're not for your horse."

Garth frantically thought of what in the world an animal could use those things for. "Well, my shepherd. She's getting old, sometimes she's incontinent, so I use them to keep her from slinging urine every time she wags her tail," he said with relief, thinking, Yeah, that sounds good.

The woman looked as if she didn't believe him.

"You just cut a hole in the, um, the backs, I guess, for the tail, put them on, and the dog has its own set of underpants." Garth was silently praying, God, get me out of here.

The woman seemed pleased with this. "Well, law, I never would have thought of that. Thad must have told you to do that."

"Yeah. Good old Thad, you can always count on him," Garth said lamely. He directed his attention to the register operator, who was asking for his money. He gladly handed her a twenty and waited impatiently for his change, then stuffed it into his pocket. He mumbled goodbye to anyone and everyone, grabbed his purchases, and took off, cursing Thad all the while.

Garth told Thad about the woman at the register and his explanation for the items he had bought, just in case she brought the subject up next time she saw him.

Thad laughed. "Hey, you'd make a good vet."

Garth nodded. "I think the underpants idea is a good one. Nothing more aggravating than having an incontinent dog sling urine all over you with their tail. Can't let my shepherd in the house anymore because of that."

"You could buy the pills, you know."

"Hey, I love my animals, okay? But spending two dollars a day for a pill just to keep the durn dog from leaking is a bit much for my budget."

"Yeah, that's what they all say." Thad snatched up the bag from Wal-Mart and headed to the bedroom.

Garth stayed behind in the kitchen while his friend tended to their patient.

"She's still out," Thad said, when he joined him. "Probably sleep through till morning. She's lost a lot of blood, but not a critical amount, I don't think. She's going to be awful weak for awhile and will need some care. You probably still ought to consider taking her to a hospital."

Garth didn't want to have to even think about dealing with Tony Salvatori. "Let's wait and see how she is tomorrow."

"In the meantime, you got anything she can use for a nightie?" Thad asked, grinning.

Garth remained silent while he considered this.

"Like maybe a t-shirt or something?" Thad nudged.

"Oh, sure." Garth found a clean thermal undershirt in the laundry room and gave it to Thad, who disappeared into the guest bedroom once more.

"Did it fit?" Garth asked when he returned to the kitchen.

"Big as you are, it makes a nice nightgown." Thad grabbed his coat and left.

CHAPTER 3

▼

Thad showed up early the next morning. Garth had checked on their patient when he rose, but she seemed to be sleeping peacefully, so he closed the bedroom door, hoping she wouldn't hear him moving around and awaken.

Thad stomped into the kitchen, approached the large, open, stone fireplace, and held his hands close to the blazing logs, warming them. "She up yet?"

"Still asleep." Garth grabbed a mug out of the cupboard, filled it from the coffeepot, and handed it to his friend.

Thad took a sip, put the cup down on the breakfast bar, and removed his coat. "You figured out what you're going to do with her?"

"Keep her here until she's well, I guess," Garth said, refilling his own cup.

Thad had a worried look on his face. "There any great chance that Salvatori guy can track her here?"

Garth glanced at him. "I guess we'll find that out," he said, hoping not.

Thad pulled out a barstool, sat down, and began unlacing his boots. "You know anything about her?"

Garth thought. "I've been trying to recall what all was said about her when I was with KPD. All I remember is she was a real enigma to our guys. All of a sudden Salvatori had this beautiful, young wife who just seemed to come from nowhere. I remember the guys called her Rapunzel because she was always so inaccessible. They couldn't approach her no matter how many times they tried or who they sent in. The only time they ever actually saw her was when Salvatori was with her, and he was protective to the max, wouldn't let anybody near her."

Garth was silent for a moment, thinking. "This guy, he's smart enough to know who he can control and who he can't and how to go about doing it. He's into politics in East Tennessee in a pretty heavy way. Our own guys were paranoid, not knowing who he had in his back pocket. There were rumors he controlled someone in the upper echelons of the mayor's office, but that was never confirmed. From time to time, KPD would try to infiltrate his organization, you know, send in someone undercover. Never worked. He found them out every time, signaling to us someone within our own department was being controlled."

Garth sat down on the stool opposite Thad. "I remember we had this one guy, Tommy, a young, go-getter kind of guy everybody liked. Well, Tommy went in, actually stayed the longest. In fact, if I remember right, he had sent word he was going to try to bring Salvatori's wife out, thought he could convince her to testify against him, but then the guy just disappeared. All we could figure was that Salvatori found him out, too."

"He killed him," they heard from the doorway. Garth and Thad looked up to see the young woman standing in the threshold with a blanket wrapped around her. Her face was as pale as diluted cream and she was swaying slightly. Both men rose to their feet and moved toward her.

Thad took her elbow and guided her into the kitchen. Garth pulled a wooden chair away from the gleaming pine table and helped Thad ease her into it.

Boo rose from his place in front of the fireplace, trotted over to where the woman was sitting, and began the sniffing process. She absently offered him her palm to smell, then caressed his head with a shaking hand.

She looked at Garth. "Tommy was my friend," she said in a miserable voice. "Tony found out who he was, so he killed him." She closed her eyes and tears trickled from each corner and ran down her face. She didn't bother wiping at them. "He forced me to watch while he beat him to death with a baseball bat. Said he wanted to teach me a lesson." She covered her eyes with her hands, as if to shut out this image.

Boo whined in sympathy as he rested his head in her lap.

Garth and Thad were too stunned to speak, visualizing this image. Garth finally mentally shook himself and noticed she now appeared even paler. He gave her a concerned look. "Would you like some coffee or orange juice? Something to drink?"

She pushed her hair off her forehead with a trembling hand. "Coffee would be nice."

Garth poured her a cup. "Sugar, cream?"

She turned to him. "Plenty of both."

Garth watched her a moment, struck by how beautiful she was, even in this state, then poured the coffee, doctored it, and took it to her. She reached out one hand, but it was shaking almost uncontrollably. Garth went down on one knee and held the cup to her lips while she took a sip. She drew her head back, eyes closed. "Thank you," she said in a weak voice, then opened her eyes and looked at him.

Those eyes again. Garth almost lost his balance.

She reached out with both hands. "I think I can manage now."

Garth made sure she had the cup securely in her hands before he let go.

Thad pulled out a chair, turned it around, and straddled it to face her. "So you are Angel Salvatori?"

"My name's Kendra, not Angel. Angel's the name he gave me, the name he calls me."

Garth and Thad looked at each other, then sat watching her slowly drink the coffee. She seemed to gain strength from that act and finally set the cup down, glancing at first Garth, then Thad.

"Thank you for what you did for me last night." Kendra appeared embarrassed. "If you'll just show me where my clothes are, I'll get dressed and leave."

"You're in no condition to travel," Thad said, his voice rising. "You've lost a lot of blood. You're too weak, you could die out there."

"I'm stronger than I look, and I can't stay here. I will not repay you-all by leading him to you."

They knew what she meant.

"You think he can track you here?" Garth asked.

She thought a moment. "Maybe not right away, but eventually."

Garth wondered if there was some way they could cover her trail. "Do you remember how you got here?"

She looked toward the fireplace, then glanced at Garth, and the pain in her eyes was almost readable. "I won't burden you with the details, but he's the reason for my condition."

Garth recalled the bruises on her body. "Meaning he's the one who beat you."

Kendra nodded. "They were taking me home from the hospital. Tony got held up by the doctor and told his driver to take me to the car. He left me alone while he smoked a cigarette outside, so I, well, took advantage of the situation." She paused long enough to cause Garth to begin to worry about her. She finally hitched a sigh and wiped at her eyes. "I knew he would have the police department and the sheriff's department and all his goons looking for me. I knew I didn't have much time. So I drove to a truck stop on the outskirts of Knoxville. There was a ridge behind the truck stop, and I drove the car up a dirt trail and into the woods as far as I could get it. I tried covering it with brush to hide it, then walked back to the truck stop. I asked around, found a driver going East, and he said he would give me a ride."

Kendra paused for a moment. "I lucked out with him. He told me he only makes this trip once a year. He usually is out West, but in November comes East to haul Christmas trees. He was heading to the eastern part of North Carolina, then up the coast, then back out West. If he keeps going, hopefully, they won't track me through him." She shivered and huddled deeper into her blanket.

"Can I get you anything?" Garth asked.

She shook her head. "When we got to Black Mountain, he stopped at a truck stop to get something warm to drink. This area, I don't know, there's something about it that appeals to me. I didn't want to chance being seen with him any longer, so while he was inside, I left. I thought I could hide out in the mountains, maybe find an abandoned cabin, but it was freezing. I found a church that was open and hid there the first night. The next day, I started walking and kept going until I found your barn. It looked so warm, and I only meant to stay there the night," she added, as if trying to apologize.

"You're lucky Garth found you as quick as he did," Thad said, in a low voice.

She turned to Garth. "You're Garth?"

He nodded. "And this is Thad. He's the one who doctored you."

Kendra gave them a miserable look. "I'm sorry I've caused you both so much trouble..."

"You didn't," Garth interrupted.

"...but I have to leave."

"You're not well enough to leave," Garth said.

"I'll be fine." Her voice was shaky.

"If what you're telling us is true, he's probably still looking for you in Tennessee," Garth said. "I don't see how he can track you here."

"You don't know him. He can do anything."

"How long have you been gone?" Garth asked.

She frowned, thinking. "This is Friday, isn't it? I didn't lose any time, did I?"

"No. Today's Friday."

"Since Wednesday afternoon; almost two days."

Garth turned to Thad. "Have you heard anything from anybody? Heard of anyone asking questions, poking around?"

Thad thought. "No, not at all."

Garth looked at her. "Thad's a nurse practitioner and also acts as veterinarian since we don't have one in this area. He gets around a lot, sees a lot of people in one day. If anyone's out there looking for you, he'd hear about it."

Thad nodded. "That's true."

"So you're safe for now," Garth said.

"I haven't seen it in the papers or heard it on the news," Thad said.

Kendra shook her head. "Tony doesn't work that way. He won't use the media. He'll use his own resources."

Garth gently took her cup, refilled and doctored it, then gave it back to her.

Kendra gave him a weak smile.

Jesus, he thought, looking at her, not wanting her to leave in this condition, wanting to protect her.

She sipped the coffee and seemed lost in her own thoughts.

Garth busied himself making another pot of coffee.

Kendra finally put the cup on the table and tried to stand, but her legs seemed to buckle. Thad caught her and eased her back into the chair.

"If I could just sleep a little more, then I'll go," Kendra said in a weak voice. She looked at Garth and tears glistened in her eyes. "I am so sorry to involve y'all in this. I would not dare ask you to help me further. I would understand if you wanted to take me somewhere, someplace he could find me."

"You're fine here," Garth said, in a stubborn manner. He picked her up, amazed at how light she felt.

"I can't have another person's death on my conscience," Kendra said, crying weakly. "Please, don't put yourself at peril, not for me. I'm not worth it."

"You're staying." Garth carried her to the bedroom. She was asleep by the time he gently lay her on the bed and covered her.

Thad gave Garth a frustrated look when he returned to the kitchen.

"What?" Garth asked, irritated by this.

"You might want to rethink this. Consider who her husband is, the type of man he is, what he might do if he tracks her here."

This made Garth angry. "What the hell do you want me to do, Thad? Call him up, say, hey, buddy, I got your wife, come get her, you didn't finish the job, she's still alive?"

Thad remained silent.

"You saw the bruises on her body, you saw what he did to her. I can't let her go back to that."

"She's not your responsibility."

"She is if I make her."

Thad studied his friend in silence.

Garth sighed. "Listen, if this makes you nervous, just stay away from here until I can get her somewhere safe, okay? You don't have to be involved in this. You've done enough already as it is. Just do me one favor, though. Don't tell anyone else about her."

Thad was shaking his head. "You think I can just walk away from this? Okay, I admit, it's got me a little scared, this guy, knowing what he's capable of. But I can't turn my back on her, either. I think maybe we should take her somewhere else, someplace safer."

Garth gave him an incredulous look. "Where exactly would that be? I mean, the way I see it, this is the safest place for her, at least for now. I don't see how he could possibly track her through that truck driver. It'd be an absolute miracle if he did. And we're a whole state away from him, on top of a mountain, for God's sake. Which, by the way, if the forecast holds true, will be impassable within the next forty-eight hours."

Thad gave him a serious look. "Just do me one favor, my friend. Be aware, all right? Be ready, in case he shows."

"I'll be ready," Garth said in a solemn tone.

CHAPTER 4

▼

Tony Salvatori, formerly Anthony Simpkins, was a ruggedly handsome man in his mid forties, tall and powerfully built with dark features and skin that appeared perpetually tanned. Tony had learned as a child that his size could be an insurmountable attribute to certain obstacles. Had come to realize fairly quickly that size could dominate, and then, later in life, an even more powerful form of intimidation, domination was his mind. He had chosen the name Tony Salvatori, exploiting the American myth concerning organized crime and Italians. He had been right.

Born into a lower middle-class family, Tony decided early on in life that he would not live as his parents had, working hard, living from paycheck to paycheck, frantically and desperately trying to make ends meet. He had gleaned from the media that drugs and crime seemed to be an easy enough, albeit somewhat lazy, means to gain financial independence, and this aspiration was Tony's motivating force.

Tony began dealing drugs as a young teenager to his neighborhood and schoolmates. He appreciated the funds to be made and, even more so, the respect his position garnered from someone half out of their mind with lust for just one hit. However, he was smart enough to never indulge in his wares and grew to hate those he looked upon as weak who did not possess the self-discipline to stay away from toxic and addictive substances.

Tony learned very early on that any show of violence in front of others of his ilk gained him the respect he felt he so richly deserved. He adopted a macho façade, appearing to not be afraid of anyone or anything, and this subterfuge quickly became ingrained into his personality. He very much liked seeing the look of dread come into another's eyes at sight of him. Liked their fear of him. Liked the way their voice would tremble if he so deigned to address them.

Tony had built his reputation on his violent nature and lack of compassion and was now head of his own organization, something he had once dreamed of being, having expanded into moving firearms, gambling and, of course, prostitution. He did not realize how much of a cliché he had come to be; would have been angered at the fact that anyone would have thought him as such.

Although he was rumored to be, he was not connected to the Mafia. But they knew of him and had come to terms with him, each agreeing to not interfere with the other's business. They didn't want to war with someone as vindictive as Tony Salvatori, knowing how powerful he had become. Besides, he was down in Tennessee, what did they care? As long as he stayed out of their business, they were happy.

Tony had, either through deception or generosity, garnered loyalty from powerful people, and the tentacles of his omnipotence stretched as far north as Washington, D.C. and as far south as Miami, Florida. He literally had infiltrated most of the police and sheriff departments within Tennessee. Finding a bad cop who could be made vulnerable was the easiest thing in the world to Tony.

When Angel had run away, Tony had sent out word that his wife was missing, giving no explanation, assuming most would presume she had been kidnapped. He let it be known he did not want the media or law enforcement officially involved, the implication being that he did not want the negotiating over the ransom to be interfered with, that he wanted to handle this on his own. However, money began to filter out amongst his loyal puppets, sending word that they were to quietly and discretely begin their own investigation, no matter what the cost, to find his Angel. There was a great rush to be the first to find Tony Salvatori's wife, simply because Tony would owe that person a huge favor, one which could not be easily repaid.

Tony was in a black mood. He sat alone in his study, trying to figure out where the hell his wife could have gotten to and so quickly. She had no family he knew of, no friends; he had made sure of that. Had no money on her, he was pretty sure of that. Dressed only in jeans and a sweater, in this cold weather, she couldn't have gone far. All he could figure was she had somehow found someone to feel sorry for her who would take her in and help her.

Angel had been gone for almost two days now and nobody in this God-forsaken city had been able to garner even the slightest clue where she could have gone. Even the damn car hadn't been sighted anywhere in East Tennessee or the surrounding states, for that matter.

Tony was troubled by the fact that she could have sold the car for money to an independent, someone who might not register it right away, delaying their tracing it through that means.

"Angel, baby, just wait till I get my hands on you this time," Tony muttered menacingly. He kicked out at his desk and cursed under his breath. Leaning his head back and closing his eyes, Tony thought of her, his Achilles heel.

Even though he was angry with her for running away as she had, he was concerned for her health and safety. She had just lost the baby; there would be loss of blood. She had no heavy clothing to protect her from the frigid weather. However, he refused to let his thoughts dwell on the fact that she could be hurt somewhere or worse, knowing his fear for her could drive him to the point of madness. He had to think clearly now, had to focus on where she could be and go get her.

Tony sighed and wearily rubbed at his eyes. His credo before Angel had been to never let himself become emotionally involved with another, to not allow himself to become vulnerable through love for another. But he had been smitten with her from the start, when she was just a skinny kid of ten running around on her father's farm. Loved the way her eyes lit up at the sight of him, loved the way she would excitedly run to him, eager to see him, always giving him a hug. Even at that age, she had been a beauty, with chestnut-colored hair, dark-gray eyes framed with heavy black lashes, slenderly built with long, coltish legs. He had given her the nickname Angel because he found her so lovely, so innocent, so pure.

Tony had known from the moment he first set eyes upon Angel that she was the one he would marry. Even more appealing to him was the fact that he could mold her, make her into the wife he wanted her to be.

But that had not been as easy as he had initially thought. He cursed himself for the thousandth time over the fact that she had learned of her mother's death and blamed him for it. He knew she suspected he had something to do with her father's disappearance, which he did, but had made sure she would never know about; punishment to her father for letting the secret out about her mother.

Okay, and the Tommy thing, he had to admit to himself he should have handled that in a better way. But damnit, she had to be taught a lesson, didn't she? She had to know whom she was dealing with here. Fat lot of good it had done him, though, because here she was, running off by herself this time.

Although Tony would never admit this to anyone, only rarely would to himself, usually while in a drunken state, the one thing on earth he longed for was his Angel to look at him the way she used to, see her eyes light up, watch her face smile with delight. But since she had learned of her mother, that light had gone out of her eyes and she rarely looked his way. Even though he doted on her, sent her fresh flowers every day, bought her anything she needed or wanted, made sure to spend time each day with her, when she would turn her gaze upon him, the only thing he saw in her eyes was accusation.

Unlike all the others, she would not let him completely dominate her, and although this irritated him mightily, he also highly respected her for it. If she were angry, she would confront him, knowing the outcome, knowing he would not tolerate this sort of defiance, knowing she would be punished. But he would look into her eyes and only then see the one passion she chose to display with him: anger. And even though he would feel remorseful after he had dealt with her for disobeying him, he managed to convince himself time after time that she only got what she had asked for. She had to be kept in line; she was his wife, after all.

Tony had contemplated for hours on how he could get Angel's love back, what he could do, but nothing seemed to work with her. Of course, she would from time to time bring up the divorce issue, but he had let her know there would be no divorce between them and made sure she was always guarded, never in a position to get away from him.

So, they had come to terms in a way. She would be his wife in public, but no further. Of course, occasionally, he would grow tired of his mistresses and whores and go to her bed, only to be rejected. This was another sore spot with him, that his wife seemed not to care for him physically, would not allow herself to partake of the pleasure he could bring her, which so many other women seemed to wantonly want from him.

But he had to admit, she had held up her end of the bargain. She was an excellent wife in public. He loved to show her off. It pleased him the way other men would stare hungrily at her, the looks of envy cast his way. She was intelligent, smarter than he, and he delighted in hearing her speak in another's foreign tongue, being fluent in Spanish, French, and German.

She had also helped to change his image somewhat, at least to the unsuspecting public. Although it annoyed him she devoted so much of her time to charities, he had become known as a generous benefactor through her doings. She was constantly hosting dinners for different charity organizations, was active in the Special Olympics and Junior Olympics. Once a week, she had handicapped children to their estate and she and other volunteers would walk them around on horses. Even though her charities were expensive, he could afford it, but, much more, appreciated the public image this afforded him.

The study door opened, interrupting Tony's musings. His driver, Vincent, stepped into the room, giving Tony a guarded look. Tony waited patiently for

Vinnie to address him, taking note of the bruises on the man's swollen face, thinking he had let Vinnie off easy for his indiscretion when he left Angel alone in the car. He had had to contain the urge to kill the man, his most loyal employee. But he had to be taught a lesson. A hard lesson. Both for his benefit and the others.

"Still no sign of her or the car," Vincent said warily, standing in front of Tony's desk.

Tony sat back, studying him. It pleased him to know a man such as Vinnie, who he had seen commit murder in cold blood without the blink of an eye, without even thinking about it really, would fear him as he did. Tony decided to edge that up a notch or two. His voice calm, his eyes deadly, he said, "You don't find something by tomorrow, Vinnie, you're dead. You understand?"

Vincent glanced at him, then away. "I'll find her."

Tony waved his hand in the air in a dismissive gesture. "Go."

Vincent quietly closed the door behind him, making sure to keep his face neutral, to not relay the disgust he felt for the man until he was safely out of his sight. He stood outside the door, considering. If Tony knew, even suspected, he had deliberately left Angel alone, knowing she would run, Vincent would die a horrible, tortuous death. Vincent, like Tony, held Angel in high regard. She was the only one he had ever known to defy Tony time after time. Even though she had to know what was coming if she refused to do what he wanted her to, she would defiantly look at her husband, eyes glaring, open her mouth, and utter the one word she knew was liable to put her in the hospital. Vincent appreciated her backbone, although he never told anyone else this. And after what Tony had done to his wife, after he had deliberately killed the child within her body, his own flesh and blood, Vincent, who had not felt empathy for anyone in years and would have been unable to identify the feeling he had for Angel as such, took pity on her. He was surprised to find his loyalty had shifted from his boss to his boss's wife. When the chance arose for her to run, he gave it to her, knowing the consequence.

Vincent moved away from the door, wondering if Tony meant what he had just now threatened, his mind weighing it out. He knew he was considered Tony's right hand, his most loyal employee; was Tony's personal bodyguard as well as driver. However, Tony had this thing about using others as examples to his minions. Vincent's indiscretion would make a fine example to be exploited, he was sure. Yet, Vincent kept the subordinates in line, kept Tony's life running smoothly. He finally decided, knowing Tony, it would depend on the mood he was in at the time. Since there was nothing he could do about it, he pushed the thought out of his mind and concentrated on a plausible plan to formulate and put into action, something to lead Tony away from his wife, to keep him from finding her. Vincent knew eventually they would have to locate her or his life would be in jeopardy, but for now, that could wait.

CHAPTER 5

▼

After checking on their patient and ascertaining she wasn't in imminent danger, Thad left to tend to his practice. Garth remembered he had forgotten to feed the horses the night before and that they were still in their stalls. He pulled on his coat, opened the outer door, and waited expectantly for his dog to join him.

"Boo!" Garth called. "Come on boy, let's go feed the horses." He was surprised the dog hadn't come running at the sound of the door swinging open. Boo was always ready to go outside with his master, in fact, hated to be left behind in the house and would throw one hell of a hissy fit if he were.

When he didn't hear paws padding across the hardwood floor in answer to his command, Garth went in search of the animal. He found him lying in the doorway of the guest bedroom, his head resting on his paws, staring at the sleeping woman. Boo looked at Garth as he approached but made no move to rise.

"You want to go outside?" Garth waited for the dog's Pavlovian response to this question, which would be to bark loudly, eagerly jump around, and excitedly rush for the door. Boo stayed on the floor.

Garth knelt down, picked up his head, and studied him. "You okay, boy?" he asked, wondering if the dog were sick or something.

Boo moved his head out of Garth's hands and looked toward the woman. Garth followed his gaze, thinking, What is this, first the horse and now the dog?

He nodded. "Okay. I'm going to go feed the horses and open their stalls in case they want to go out. I won't be gone long."

Boo placed his head back on his paws and made a groaning noise deep in his throat as if to say, "Don't let me stop you."

"I won't," Garth answered.

Garth stayed outside longer than he intended, feeding the animals, breaking the thin layer of ice that had formed on top of the water trough, mucking out the stalls, then cutting firewood to bring inside. He would occasionally glance up at the sunroom, expecting to see Boo at the bank of windows, watching him, waiting to be let out, but only saw a dismal sun swimming behind racing gray-hued streaks of clouds reflected in the panes. He would occasionally stop and listen, expecting to hear Boo at the back door barking loudly and furiously, tearing away at this barrier, angry that he was still inside while Garth was outside, but was only met with silence.

He entered the house, carrying a load of firewood, half-expecting to be met at the door by the big dog and knocked down as punishment for not letting him out, but was only met with hushed stillness. Huh! Garth thought, going into the sunroom and putting the wood in the wood box by the hearth. After shrugging out of his coat, he walked down the hall toward the guest room.

Boo was there, in the same place, patiently watching over the sleeping woman. Kendra had now been joined by Garth's cat, a calico-colored Persian curled up against her stomach.

Garth shook his head as he walked back to the kitchen, expecting to be followed, but not. Huh! he thought once more, glancing around behind him. Well, he knew what got their attention. He fished a can of soup out of the cupboard, took it to the automatic can opener, placed it on the spool, and turned it on. He looked toward the hallway as the opener made its grinding noise. Neither animal appeared. Garth was stunned. If that durn dog and, okay, the cat was just as bad, suspected there was food anywhere at anytime, they both came running, expecting to share the bounty.

Garth dumped the soup into a pan, added water, turned on the gas flame, and waited for the food to boil, constantly glancing toward the doorway. When the soup began bubbling, he poured some into a large coffee mug and walked toward the bedroom.

Neither the cat nor the dog had moved. Garth scowled at them as he stepped into the room. Kendra seemed to sense him and opened her eyes sleepily, then gave him a weak smile when she had focused on him.

Garth felt his heart lurch as he walked toward her. "I thought you might be hungry, so I made you some soup."

Kendra feebly sat up and brushed the hair out of her eyes and away from her face. She noticed the cat, which had been usurped from its nest when she shifted and had moved close to the edge of the bed, regarding her with solemn eyes.

"Hey, beauty." Kendra put a still-shaky hand on the cat's head and stroked down its body. The cat responded by standing on all fours and arching its back.

Boo, always jealous of anyone or anything getting more attention than he, rose on all fours and padded over to Kendra. He rested his head on the bed and looked at her with his strange eyes.

She smiled with delight, albeit infirmly. Garth couldn't help but grin in response.

"Look at you," she cooed to the dog. She glanced at Garth. "A Weimaraner?"

"Not many people know the breed."

"Oh, I love these dogs. German hunters brought over by Eisenhower."

Garth was impressed.

"They call these ghost eyes, don't they?"

"Yeah, some do."

She scratched behind the dog's ears. "What's your name, big boy?"

Boo made a low, rumbling noise in his throat as if in answer.

"Boo Radley," Garth interpreted.

She glanced at him. "The character in 'To Kill a Mockingbird,'" she correctly surmised. She cupped Boo under the chin, brought her face close to his and said, "You don't scare me. You've got a gentle soul, I can tell." This was met with Boo's wet tongue, causing her to smile.

"All right, Sarge, get off the bed." Garth shooed the cat away, pulled over the desk chair, nudged Boo aside, and sat, facing her.

"Thad said to keep you on the light stuff for a day or two, so I thought soup might do the trick." Garth held the mug toward her.

"I'm famished," Kendra said, reaching for it.

Garth noticed she now appeared waxen. He could see beads of sweat on her upper lip and forehead, and became worried that the simple act of talking could tire her out so quickly. "Here, let me hold the cup for you. It's kind of heavy." He brought it to her lips and she placed her hands around his, guiding the cup, then moved it away after taking a couple of swallows.

Kendra leaned back, looking paler than ever. "That's good." She gave him a gracious smile.

Garth smiled. "Can't do better than Campbell's Chicken Noodle." He waited patiently for her to let him know she was ready for more.

It took a long while and some coaxing on his part, but Garth got her to drink most of the soup. He could tell by her movements she was in pain and encouraged her to take two ibuprofen. He had to hold the glass of water for her while she drank.

Kendra finally lay back, exhausted. "Thank you so much."

Garth noticed there were tears brimming in her eyes. "Hey," he said, surprised.

"You're so kind, Garth." She closed her eyes and her voice grew sleepy. "I don't think I've ever met anyone so kind."

Garth tucked the covers comfortably around her, then left the room, after having to step over the damn dog, who had resumed playing sentinel at the doorway.

CHAPTER 6

▼

Kendra slept the afternoon. Garth kept himself busy in the sunroom, working on a western saddle he was restoring, checking on her from time to time. It amused and confused him the way the dog was acting toward her, as if he were her own personal bodyguard. Not to mention the cat, who usually liked hanging around with Garth, but who now seemed to prefer sleeping against the woman's stomach. Boo, who was constantly running in and out of the house like a two-year-old if the weather wasn't too bad, only wanted out once, did his business, came right back in, glanced at Garth, then took off down the hallway to the bedroom.

"Nice to know who your friends are," Garth called after him, which Boo ignored.

Mid-afternoon, Garth threw together enough ingredients to make homemade soup, something with substance this time. When it grew dark, he opened the kitchen door in order to go outside to bed down the horses and waited for Boo to join him. When the dog didn't appear, Garth called for him, but Boo ignored him. So Garth went outside by himself, realizing as he trudged toward the barn how much he depended on that dang dog for companionship. "I gotta get a life," he mumbled to himself, as he entered the shelter.

Back inside, Garth made cornbread to go with the soup and was just taking it out of the oven when he felt more than heard movement. He glanced up to see Kendra, the dog, and the cat standing in the kitchen doorway watching him.

"Hope you're hungry," he told her with a smile. He tucked a case knife between the cornbread and the inside of the iron skillet, then ran it around the circumference.

"Smells wonderful," Kendra said, walking toward him.

Garth noticed her face was slightly flushed, but her walk seemed sturdier. She sat down at the breakfast bar and wrapped the blanket around her.

"You want to eat at the bar?" Garth put the knife down, picked up oven mitts, and turned the skillet upside down over a plate, dumping the cornbread.

"Please." Kendra reached down to pet Boo, who was now sitting beside her. The cat jumped up on the stool next to her and climbed over onto her lap.

"What's with you and animals?" Garth couldn't help but ask, thinking of the way the horse had offered her his body heat the evening before.

She shrugged her shoulders. "I've always loved domesticated animals. I think maybe they have better souls than we humans do." She pet Boo with one hand, Sarge with the other. Both animals gazed at her in an adoring way.

Garth fixed Boo's food and placed it on the floor near the door, where the dog always ate, then opened Sarge a can of cat food, his nightly treat, and placed it inside the pantry so Boo couldn't get to it. Both animals stayed with Kendra.

"Damndest thing I've ever seen," Garth mumbled to himself.

"I'm sorry?"

"Nothing, just talking to myself." Garth busied himself pulling out plates and bowls and placing them on the bar.

He opened the refrigerator. "You drink milk?"

"Skim if you've got it."

"Is there any other?"

She gave a glimpse of a smile.

Garth poured milk for both of them, put the glasses on the bar, brought the large kettle of soup over and ladled food into her bowl, then his. He returned the kettle to the stove, then set the plate with the warm, golden cornbread on the bar. He took butter from the refrigerator and placed it next to the cornbread as he sat down.

Garth noticed she was watching him. "What?"

"You seem to, I don't know, be at great ease in the kitchen. I like that." Kendra's face flushed pink.

Garth grinned. "Being a bachelor, I'm kind of forced to be." He sliced the cornbread and placed a piece on her bread plate.

"You're not married?"

"Divorced."

She nodded but didn't ask questions.

"Butter?"

"Please," she said, taking it from him. Kendra buttered her cornbread, then picked up a spoon and tasted the soup. She closed her eyes. "Pure heaven."

"Does my heart good to see someone enjoy my cooking," Garth said, somewhat ironically. She smiled, although he couldn't help notice it was a sad one.

They made small talk while they ate, mostly about the weather, dogs, cats, and horses.

"I love to ride," Kendra told him with a longing look in her eyes. "I don't think there's a better, maybe freer feeling than riding a horse at full gallop, the wind hitting you in the face, that beautiful, powerful animal under you, carrying you along with it." She paused and gave him an embarrassed look. "Sorry. I'm usually not so tangential."

"Describes perfectly the way I feel about it."

They smiled at one another.

Garth thought, Damn, I could love this woman without even trying to. Realizing he was staring at her, he looked away.

After eating in silence for awhile, Kendra surprised him by saying, "We've met before, you and I."

Garth glanced at her and nodded.

"You brought—was it your nephew you brought to the Special Olympics a couple of years ago?"

Garth smiled widely. "Yeah, Jake," he said, thinking how he loved that kid; how much he missed him since he and his mother, Garth's sister, had moved away.

She returned his smile. "He was such a cutie."

Garth grinned wider. "Still is."

She studied him a moment. "Weren't you with the police department? Didn't I see you at the DARE functions?"

Garth nodded, concentrating on his food, then feeling her eyes on him, glanced at her. "I took an early retirement," he said, in a brusque voice.

Kendra seemed to catch his uneasiness and was silent for a moment as she looked around the cozy kitchen, then toward the bank of windows in the connecting sunroom framing a panoramic mountainous view. "Well, you sure picked the perfect place to retire to, Garth," she observed.

Garth smiled.

When she was finished, Kendra told him once more how much she appreciated what all he had done for her. "If you could just show me where my clothes are..."

Garth gave her a stern look. "You're not leaving."

They stared at one another for several moments. He could see the battle she was having within herself, could see she really didn't want to leave, and allowed himself to fleetingly wonder if it was because of her health or some other reason. Then thought how stupid that was; she had only just met him.

Kendra finally nodded. "Okay, not tonight. I'm still weak as a kitten. But I would like to take a shower, if that's all right. And I need to change my, uh, underwear and this t-shirt you let me sleep in, so if I could just have my clothes, I'll put them back on."

"Your jeans and sweater were caked with blood and Thad had to cut them off you, along with your, uh, underwear. It was, well, stuck to your skin in places, and he had to soak parts of it off." Garth's face felt red. He glanced at her and noticed she was also blushing.

She nodded. "And the underwear I'm wearing now?"

Garth made a face, then told her the story of how that came to be. He smiled when she smiled, even wider when she laughed at the young girl calling him a pervert, thinking that was the first time she had laughed, noticing the sad look which seemed stamped on her face was momentarily gone when she did. He was surprised at the ease he felt with this woman, something he had experienced with very few people in his life.

When he had finished, Kendra said, her voice full of wonder, "You're my hero, you know that?"

Garth thought she might be teasing him, but looking into her eyes, could see her sincerity. He cleared his throat. "There's more underwear in the dresser drawer in the bedroom. The, uh, pads…"

"I found those in the bathroom earlier," she interrupted.

Garth nodded. "As for something to wear, my sister, Jake's mother, has some clothes she leaves here for when she visits. I think you're about her size. They're packed away, but I'll pull them out and wash them for you. In the meantime, I have some sweats you can wear if you want; you know, a fleece shirt and pants. They're warm, probably way too big, but the pants have a drawstring, so you should be able to make them fit."

Kendra rose, slightly wobbly now. "That would be great."

Garth stood, came around, and steadied her. "Maybe you ought to take a bath, not a shower," he said, worried she would fall.

She leaned against him a moment. "Yes, a hot bath would be wonderful."

Garth helped her to the bathroom and showed her where the towels and wash-cloths were. He got a pair of fresh underwear for her, then the sweats he had promised, along with a pair of white, cotton socks, and knocked on the bathroom door. After she called for him to come in, he opened the door. Kendra was sitting on the side of the tub, letting it fill with steamy water, wearing only the t-shirt.

Her face was flushed and glistening with perspiration, causing him to wonder if it was from the humidity in the bathroom or something else. Please, God, don't let her get sick, please don't let this be sign of a fever, he silently prayed.

Garth placed the clothing on the vanity. "If you need anything else, just holler." He made a hasty retreat, cursing himself for the sexual thought nudging at his brain that he would love to be in that tub with her, love to wash her body, feel her body…Wondering where in the hell that had come from.

"Stop it," he mumbled to himself, returning to the kitchen to begin the cleanup. He noticed the dog and cat had decided they'd join him and were eating their food. "Traitors," he snarled at them. Each gave him an indulgent look, then resumed eating.

Kendra was in the bath a long while. Garth approached the bathroom door twice, intending to knock and ask if she were all right, but hearing movement, decided not to interrupt her.

When she joined him, her face was rosy pink and damp. She had washed and towel-dried her hair, and it hung loosely around her shoulders. The sweatshirt came to mid thigh, the pants were wadded around her ankles, and, of course, the heels of the socks rode up the backs of her legs. She looked more beautiful to him than anything he had ever seen. Garth had to suppress speaking this thought to Kendra as she stood in the doorway to the sunroom, her hand idly landing on Boo's head, who had gone to her. Garth noticed the cat was lazily twirling in and out between her feet.

Kendra gave him a shy smile. "I think I'm going to go lie down." Her voice sounded weak. "I'm awfully tired, but thank you for…"

"Enough with the thank yous," Garth interrupted, going to her. "Here, let me help you." He took her arm and guided her to the bedroom, then tucked covers around her after she was reclining.

"You're very maternal," she murmured, closing her eyes.

He stiffened.

She seemed to sense this. "I meant that as the highest form of compliment you can give a man."

"Well, then, thanks." Garth watched the cat jump onto the bed and snuggle against her stomach. Kendra's hand immediately stroked the furry animal and a loud purring sound emitted at her touch.

Garth almost tripped over the Boo-dog, who was standing guard at the doorway. He decided to keep the door open so the dang dog and cat could get out if they needed to.

He checked the bathroom to see if he needed to do any sort of cleanup, but Kendra had tidied up herself. Garth breathed in her sweet female scent, liking the way the bathroom smelled, wondering what it was about a woman that could change the feel of a room, simply by the simple feat of being there. He returned to the sunroom and decided to turn on the TV to listen to the local news, see if there was anything being broadcast about his houseguest.

CHAPTER 7

▼

Vincent sat in Tony's office, smoking a cigarette, listening to his boss harangue one of his many contacts within the police department. Tony was irritated the car hadn't been located yet and was doing a lot of cursing and threatening.

Mark, one of the newer recruits whose job it had been to guard Kendra, knocked on the door. Vincent stood and answered it.

Mark looked happy. "We just got a call from some guy in Chattanooga. Says they have a black Lexus down there, same model as Tony's, found it when they raided a chop shop this morning."

Tony had hung up the phone and was listening to this. "Is it mine?" he asked, standing, his eyes glistening.

Mark glanced at Vincent, then to Tony. "They can't tell us. The license plate's gone, the serial number's been burned off. But he described it to me, and it sure as hell sounds like yours."

Vincent watched Tony process this, relieved at the distraction this would offer.

Tony turned to Vincent. "Chattanooga's what, an hour and a half drive, right?"

Vincent nodded, stubbing out his cigarette in the ashtray on Tony's desk, blowing twin pillars of smoke out his nose.

Tony addressed Mark. "Call that guy back and get directions to this place. Tell him to hold it till we get there. We're leaving now."

Mark nodded and backed out of the room.

The man who had made the call was waiting on them at the chop shop: a young, baby-faced state trooper with rust-colored hair and freckles covering his face, arms, and hands. Vincent fleetingly wondered exactly how many dirty cops Tony had working for him as he braked to a stop.

The man smiled widely when they pulled into the lot, acting proud of himself. He opened Tony's door for him, waited for him to climb out, then closed it. "I think this is the car you're looking for, sir," he said with reverence.

"Where is it?" Tony asked.

"Around back. Don't worry. Nobody's touched it since I called." He led them past the decrepit stone building from which the illegal establishment had functioned.

Vincent stopped when he saw the car, thinking, Nope, already preparing himself for what he knew was coming.

Tony turned and glanced at Vincent, his expression dark and ominous. He approached the car and looked it over.

The trooper was smiling widely. "Well?"

"Did you even bother to read the description of the car, you dick-head?" Tony raved at him.

The young man seemed to shrink a little and darted looks at Vincent, then Tony. "It said a black Lexus. It matches the model numbers given on the sheet."

Tony stalked toward him, giving him a rageful glare. "What else did the sheet say?"

The trooper looked like he didn't know how to respond to that.

"What'd it say about the interior? You remember what it said?"

"Leather seats. Fully decked out, CD player, GPS system, the works."

"What kind of leather'd it say? Did you bother to read that?" Tony screamed at him.

The trooper backed away. "Leather's leather."

Tony grabbed the man by the collar, pulled him over to the car, and opened the driver's door. "What kind of leather's that?" He shoved his face in the seat, then pulled him up. "What the hell kind of leather is that?"

The trooper cast his eyes beseechingly at Vincent. His look changed to severe disappointment when he realized there would be no help from that corner. "I don't know, man. I didn't know there were different kinds of leather."

Tony threw him against the car. "The sheet says Corinthian leather. You ever heard of Corinthian leather? That crap in that car's nothing but plastic."

The young man cowered against the vehicle, looking frightened, not saying anything, afraid to.

Tony pulled his gun.

Vincent flinched, thinking, Damn.

Tony shot out the right rear tire, then the front. He approached the trooper and fired past his head into the front seat. The trembling officer screamed and covered his head as stuffing lazily puffed into the air, reminding Vincent of tiny cirrus clouds. Tony shot the dashboard, then the passenger seat. He finally brought the gun to bear on the trooper, who was cringing and crying like a baby.

"You deliver this message for me," Tony said, his voice low, deadly. "You tell these cowboys out here I get sent on anymore wild-goose chases, the next guy's gonna end up in the morgue." He shot the trooper in the knee.

His screams were piercing.

Tony holstered his gun and walked toward Vincent, ignoring the injured man.

Vincent gave him a passive look.

"Let's go," Tony said, walking back to the car.

CHAPTER 8

▼

Garth had spent the afternoon outside, preparing for the blizzard the forecasters were predicting. When he entered the house, he found Kendra in the sunroom, sitting in the large, overstuffed chair next to the windows, staring out at the mountains. He was relieved to see she was up; he hoped that meant she was feeling better. The past week, she had seemed to do nothing but sleep unless he woke her to eat or when Thad came to check on her progress.

When she noticed he was in the room, she startled a bit, then wiped quickly at her eyes.

"I didn't mean to disturb you." Garth placed more logs on the dwindling fire in the open fireplace that stood between the sunroom and the kitchen.

Kendra gave him a weak smile. "It's okay. I'm just feeling a bit melancholy, I'm afraid." Her eyes traveled away from him.

Garth noticed her hand had come to rest on her stomach. "It's all right to mourn your baby. It's only natural to grieve over that loss," he said in a gentle voice.

Kendra put her hands over her face.

"I'm sorry." Garth put his hand on her shoulder. "I didn't mean to upset you."

She shook her head and wiped at her eyes. "You didn't."

Garth sat down on the ottoman facing her, wondering what in the world had happened to this woman to bring her to this point.

Kendra glanced up, caught him watching her.

"Would it help to talk about what happened?"

"I probably owe you that much," Kendra said in a subdued voice.

"Not if you don't want to. You don't have to tell me anything."

"I think I'd like to, though." She stared out at the mountains once more. After a few moments, Garth was just about to rise, to leave her alone, when she said, "When I found out I was pregnant, my first thought was, I've got to kill this child."

Garth gave her a sharp look.

She glanced at him and nodded. "It was Tony's child, his demon seed. He's evil personified; I don't think there's any good in him at all. The baby would have his genes, and I wondered, is evilness genetic? I debated that question with myself for a long time. I finally decided, yes, but the baby was also mine. I'm not evil. I do not follow his creed, I do not think like he does, feel like he does. And I began to want my baby. I wanted someone to love, someone to love me back in a normal way. So, I didn't do anything about it. I just kept my mouth shut until I was starting to show, and then I told him."

She shuddered and a sob caught in her throat. "He didn't even consider me having the baby. The first words out of his mouth were, 'I'll make an appointment with your doctor tomorrow, we'll have it taken care of.' I asked him what he meant specifically by that. He said, 'Get rid of it, of course.'"

She glanced out the windows. "I told him that's not what I wanted. He said, 'You don't have a say in this, Angel. You do what I tell you to do, and I'm not going to let this happen.'" Her voice had turned caustic, she spoke barely above a whisper.

"I asked him how could he put a death sentence on his own child who was at that very moment growing inside me. He just laughed and said he probably had a dozen babies walking around, take your pick." Her face looked tortured. "I told him I was going to have the baby, I would not have an abortion, and he had no say-so in the matter. He got mad, needless to say. Kept telling me it was his way or else, and I kept telling him no, not this time. So he did what he always did, punished me for not obeying his wishes, by beating me."

She stopped and tried to calm herself. "Oh, I got an abortion all right, one induced by Tony," she said, her voice acerbic.

"Damn bastard." Garth growled.

"I passed out, I guess, but next thing I knew, I was in the hospital. They told me they had done a D&C on me, which was standard after a spontaneous abortion." She barked a harsh laugh. "Spontaneous abortion. I almost spat in the doctor's face when he told me that. I said, 'Look at the bruises on my stomach and tell me this was spontaneous.' He just turned away. It was always that way with them, they never questioned the bruises or the contusions or the lacerations, always choosing to believe what Tony told them. I guess the fact that he made a half-million dollar contribution to their cancer ward helped."

"How the hell did you live like that?" Garth asked in a raw voice.

"When you live in a prison, you don't have any choice in the matter. I was never allowed out of his sight or the sight of my bodyguards, as he called them. Although all they were, to tell you the truth, were Tony's goons, there to make sure I didn't get away from him."

"But you did."

She gave him a brittle smile. "Yes, I did, with a little help. And if he finds me, if I go back, I'll do it again. Maybe one day, if I'm lucky, he'll be so angry with me for running away from him that he'll kill me, take me out of the hell he has created for me."

Garth regarded her, unable to believe she felt this way. "He won't get you back this time," he finally said in a low voice.

Their gazes locked.

"I'll make sure of it," he said, answering the question in her eyes.

She shook her head. "I will not trade another life for mine. I will not let that happen to you."

Garth did not voice it but made a pledge to himself that he would protect this woman, he would make sure she did not go back to the man who had committed this atrocity to her body. He would not, could not, allow her, anyone for that matter, to return to a baby-killer. Instead, he said, "You look tired. Why don't you take a nap while I fix dinner?"

She smiled at him as if relieved.

CHAPTER 9

▼

Tony had Vincent bring one of his mistresses to the estate, then dismissed him, letting him know she would be spending the night.

Vincent went off to pay a visit to his lawyer, glad to be away from his boss and his continual foul mood.

Tony was in a dour mood and felt he needed cheering up. The mistress he had instructed Vincent bring to him was the youngest of the lot, only nineteen, with auburn hair and blue eyes. Freckles all over her skin. She not only possessed a perky affect but body, as well. And she liked sex. A lot.

As Tony lay, feeling her mouth on him, his body responding, his mind dwelt on Angel. He was surprised to feel his eyes grow hot, his throat close. He roughly pushed Debra away.

She looked up at him, surprised. "What?"

"Nothing," he said brusquely, rising, walking to the minibar. He opened the good whiskey and poured a small amount into a glass. He didn't ask her if she wanted any, instead turned his back on her and knocked the dark liquid back in one swallow, immediately followed by another.

Debra sat up and watched him, aggravated he was treating her so rudely. She had heard rumors of Tony's propensity for violence, but up to this point, Tony had always treated her with care. She watched the movement of the muscles in his back as he lifted the bottle, and her eyes traveled his nude body. Although he was much older than she, Debra found him sexy as hell. He was a voracious lover, and the fact that he was wealthy made their arrangement even more appealing. She forgot her irritation with him as another thought intruded. Tony's wife was still missing. Maybe she would never be found. Tony liked being married, he had told her that enough. Thoughts of becoming the next Mrs. Tony Salvatori made her squirm with delight.

Debra rose from the bed and stealthily approached him. She hugged Tony from behind, ground her pelvis against him. "What's wrong, Tony?"

Tony shrugged out of her hold, walked to the window, drew the curtains aside, and looked out. It had been snowing heavily all day, an anomaly for November, and now that night had ousted day, the outside world glistened with the icy mixture that had begun to fall as the temperature dropped. Where the hell are you, Angel? Tony thought, staring out at the snow-covered trees and frozen roads. He was feeling frustrated, out of sorts. His worry seemed to consume him now. It was hard to concentrate on anything but where his wife could be, was she safe, was she hurt, was she lying dead somewhere. A small part of his brain knew he was responsible for this, but he chose instead to blame Angel. He clinched his fists, wished she were here, wished he could take out his frustration on her.

Debra approached Tony once more and sidled around to place herself between his body and the window. She smiled perkily at him as she ran her hands over his abdomen, then down. "Come on back to bed, Tony. I'll help you feel better."

He stepped back and slapped her, knocking her down. She crouched with one hand to her cheek, which was quickly turning red. Tears glistened in her eyes as she looked up at him.

Tony glared at her. "You want to help me feel better?" He reached down, picked her up, and threw her on the bed, ignoring her protests, followed by screams.

Vincent tried to hide his surprise at seeing Debra in Tony's office the next morning. She was squeezed into the farthest corner of the couch with her legs drawn up to her chest, visibly shaking and chewing her nails. She darted anxious looks at Tony, who sat behind his desk, on the phone, bullying one county official or another, ignoring her.

Vincent kept his face passive as he took Debra in with one glance. He wouldn't meet her swollen eyes when they tried to hold his, furtively begging him to get her away from here. Her nose appeared to be broken, her face was bruised, her throat bright red. There was dried blood around her lips. He could see welts on her upper legs, purplish bruises forming on her upper arms. Shit, he thought with disgust, wondering what in hell was wrong with his boss he had to go picking on someone who had no chance in the world going up against him.

Vincent sat in the chair across from Tony and stared out the window behind the desk. His fingers found the cigarette pack in his inside jacket pocket, without even realizing he was doing this. He tapped a cigarette out, removed it, and replaced the pack. His hand strayed into his pants pocket, fishing for his lighter. He ignored the small whimpers issuing from the girl on the couch.

After he lit up, he leaned forward, placed the lighter on Tony's desk and sat smoking, thinking. Tony was pretty much out of control now. He had always been violent, abusive with anyone who defied him or got in his way. But Vincent was betting that wasn't the case here. Probably more like misplaced anger directed away from his missing wife. He began to wonder if something shouldn't be done about the man sitting in front of him.

Tony hung up the phone, cutting off Vincent's thoughts. He glanced first at the girl, then directed his attention to his driver. "Stupid bunch of idiots," he raved, his voice low, causing Debra to shake more violently. "Couldn't find anything if it was sitting right there in front of them."

Vincent idly smoked.

Tony gave him a belligerent look. "You got any leads yet? You got any ideas in that head of yours you haven't smoked out with all those damn cigarettes you keep stuck in your mouth?"

"Getting mad at the world isn't going to get your wife back, Tony," Vincent said in a low, calm voice.

Tony stiffened.

"Beating up on somebody don't need beating up on ain't gonna do it, either," Vincent said, resorting to gutter talk.

Tony's eyes narrowed. "I ought to kill you for that."

"Yeah, but you won't." Vincent leaned forward, pulled a ceramic ashtray toward him, and stubbed out the cigarette. "After all, boss, who'd you have to clean up all the messes you keep leaving behind?" He stood, approached Debra, and extended his hand.

She reached out to him, her arms shaking so violently her hands were doing a solo dance at the end of her wrists. Vincent took her by the upper arms and helped her to stand, trying to ignore the soft, wheezing sounds issuing from her. Debra leaned against him, shaking and whimpering. Vincent turned to Tony, who remained behind the desk, glaring. "She needs to get to a hospital, Tony. Looks like you broke her nose, maybe a few ribs, the way she's wheezing."

Tony picked up the phone and swiveled around in his chair to face the window, ignoring him as he punched in a number.

Vincent half-carried, half-supported Debra to the car. He opened the door and helped her inside, scowling at the startled looks of the other men standing guard. All they had seen, you'd think they'd be use to this by now, Vincent thought as he rounded the front of the car, climbed in the driver's seat, started it up, and drove away.

As soon as they were moving, Debra began sniffling, then put her shaking hands to her face and sobbed loudly. Vincent reached out and put a hand on her shoulder. "Try not to do that, girl. It'll only hurt worse you cry like that." Damn, he had to get away from this guy. After he found Angel, that is. Okay and took care of Tony for what he did to her.

CHAPTER 10

▼

The woman's eyes were wide with horror, disbelief. She looked into his own, pleading with them to not let this man hurt her, not let her die, not like this, to not leave her. All without saying a word, all with just her eyes, which were beautiful: large, dark-gray ovals, framed with thick, ebony lashes. Eyes that would never leave him for the rest of his life. He reached out to her, was within inches of pulling her from harm, when his face was spattered with pieces of her flesh, tissue, brain; drenched with hot blood. Feeling all this before hearing the fatal shot.

Garth came awake, this time seeing those eyes before his face, but not dying. Wide awake, alive, with a frightened, worried cast.

Kendra was shaking him slightly. "Garth?"

"Jesus." He sat up and tried to control the shaking.

She was looking at him with concern. "You were having a nightmare."

He wiped the sweat from his face. "It's okay."

She watched him with a worried look.

Garth gave her a wry smile. "Sorry I woke you. Believe me, I didn't mean to."

She cocked her head and raised her eyebrows. "Chasing demons?"

He ran his hand over his face. "You could say that."

She was silent a moment. "Who's your demon, Garth?"

He looked back at her. "Me," he answered.

CHAPTER 11

▼

Kendra had been sitting in the overstuffed chair in the sunroom, staring out at the falling snow, worrying, Garth was sure. He had approached her a few times, then backed off, uncertain what to say to her. Sarge was sleeping contentedly in her lap. Boo, who was lying beside the chair, would raise his head every once in awhile, and she would idly rub behind his ears until he put his head back down on his forepaws.

Garth finally thought, Shoot, it's got to be said, so entered the sunroom, pulled the ottoman away from the chair, and sat down on it, facing her.

Kendra seemed to startle at the movement, then stared at his face, waiting.

Every time Garth looked at her, he was overwhelmed with not only the beauty she possessed but the calm, serene feeling she seemed to exude. He knew she was in turmoil, yet to the naked eye, she seemed to be at great peace with herself and her world.

He cleared his throat while continuing to hold her gaze. "Can I talk to you for a minute?"

Kendra gave him a slight smile as she nodded. Sarge raised up, stretched, turned around, and settled back in the very same position he had been. Kendra's hand moved along his back, stroking him. The cat began to purr loudly. Garth leaned toward her, resting his forearms on his thighs, and gave her an intent look. "Listen, I know you're thinking you need to leave. I can tell that's on your mind, but we need to talk about that."

Kendra frowned slightly at him and tilted her head to the side.

"Just hear me out, okay? Just listen to what I have to say."

She watched him but didn't say anything.

"As you can see, we're caught in one hell of a blizzard, the second one this month." Garth waved his hand toward the window. Kendra's eyes followed the movement of his hand, then returned to his. "I've been thinking about this, Kendra, and I have to tell you, this is probably the best place in the world for you right now."

She opened her mouth, to protest, he was sure.

"No, listen to what I want to say first, then we'll talk, okay?" he interrupted hastily. Without giving her a chance to respond to that, he continued. "We're on top of a mountain here, there's hardly any chance at all that your husband can track you through that truck driver, especially since he was going back out West, and even if he did, he'd have a hell of a time getting up here. This summit is one of the most secluded peaks in the Black Mountains range. It's virtually impassable when the snow hits, and from November till March it's just about impossible to get around. That's why so many of us own four-wheelers and horses." He stopped and rubbed his hands on his knees. "You're not well, you're still weak, you're still recovering from the—from what happened. And I think what you need to do is give yourself this time to recover, mentally as well as physically, to grieve over your baby, to get back to where you need to be before you decide what you ought to be doing." He stopped when he noticed tears in her eyes.

Kendra had been listening to him, thinking there was nothing she would love more than being able to stay in this beautiful, peaceful place her whole life, but she knew that was not possible. Too many people had died because of her, no one else would. She had decided that, feeling her baby's life slipping away inside her own. "Can I speak now?" she asked, in a shaky voice.

Garth felt uncomfortable. "I didn't mean to upset you. I just want you to know what I think is the best course of action for you right now."

Kendra nodded. "I understand." She wiped at her eyes. "But I can't stay here." She looked directly at him. "Much as I'd like to, I won't stay here, Garth. It's too risky for you. I won't chance anything happening to you because you were kind enough to help me."

He was stunned at this. Here she was, running from a killer, having suffered a miscarriage at his hands, almost dying from it, and she was worried about his safety. "I was a policeman once, I can take care of myself," he said, in a gruff voice.

She gave him a pained look. "Tommy thought the same thing."

"Tommy was a rookie. He didn't have the experience I have."

Tears were coursing down her face. "Tommy was my friend," she said, wiping angrily at her eyes. "It's my fault he died."

"He knew going in there was dangerous. He knew what he was getting himself into, he was well aware of the risks. It was his job, Kendra, something he understood."

Kendra rested her head against the back of the chair and the agony on her face was almost unbearable.

Garth resisted the urge to put his arms around her and comfort her.

"Tommy was the only friend I ever had." She paused, as if looking back at memories, and smiled slightly. "He was such a cocky guy."

Garth grinned in response. Yeah, he remembered that about Tommy, who liked to strut his stuff but had the type of personality you couldn't help but like.

"I'd go riding most days, on the estate. Tommy liked horses, too, so he'd talk to me about that. Tony didn't like me being out by myself, even though he has that place guarded better than the White House, so he decided he'd let Tommy ride with me." She smiled to herself, remembering. "Tommy was a lot of fun. I'd never had someone to converse with for any length of time. Tony always made sure of that. His driver, Vinnie, was the closest thing I had to a friend until Tommy. Vinnie likes to read, so we'd talk about books until Tony got tired of it. But with Tommy, I had hours and hours to talk about anything we wanted to talk about." Her face grew sad. "I always looked forward to those rides."

"How'd Tony find out about him?"

"I don't know. One day, we came in from riding and Tony had all his goons there. He had this wild look in his eyes and started accusing Tommy of infiltrating his organization, trying to take me away, trying to get me to testify against him. When I tried to take up for Tommy, he started accusing me of wanting to leave with him." She looked with anguish at Garth. "He made a couple of his men hold me, made me watch while he beat Tommy to death," she said, her voice hitching. "I screamed and screamed and screamed, tried to get away from them, tried to help poor Tommy." Her voice had risen and she was crying openly now.

"Hey." Garth reached out and stroked her arm.

"Then afterwards, he took me in the house, took me to my room, started beating on me. I begged him to kill me, pleaded with him. He probably would have if Vinnie hadn't stopped him." She glanced at Garth, then away. "I sometimes wish Vinnie hadn't been there." She gently picked up Sarge and placed him on the floor, then rose and went to her room, closing her door gently as if not to arouse someone sleeping.

Garth watched her leave, wondering how someone could have suffered through all that she had and still come out the other side fairly normal. He sat there for a long time, thinking. This woman was special, he knew that. He was well aware his reason for wanting her to stay went beyond his masculine need to protect her. He finally decided if he couldn't stop her from leaving, maybe he could delay her going for awhile.

He rapped on her bedroom door.

Kendra opened the door slightly and looked at him through the gap. Her eyes were red and swollen, her face ruddy.

Garth felt uncomfortable, unsure of himself. "Listen, what we were talking about before. At least promise me you'll wait until this weather breaks and you're better physically before you do anything, and I'll help you get away. I'll do anything I can to help you, if you'll just promise me that."

She regarded him for a moment, then nodded her assent and gently closed the door once more.

CHAPTER 12

▼

Kendra awoke to good smells, warm, comforting smells. Her stomach responded with growling noises, driving her into the kitchen. She stood in the doorway and watched Garth lean over the oven, basting a golden-brown turkey. "Smells great." She smiled at him as she walked toward the coffeepot.

Garth smiled back.

"What's the occasion?"

He thought she might be teasing him, but seeing her look, realized she wasn't. "Today's Thanksgiving."

She blinked in surprise. "Already?"

He nodded.

Kendra had a stunned expression on her face. "So I've been here three weeks already?"

"Just about."

Kendra stood, lost in thought.

"Don't even think about it."

She looked at him. "What?"

"Leaving. We talked about that before and I'd appreciate it if you'd just stick with the plan we agreed on."

"The plan was I'd leave when I was better and the weather broke. The snow's cleared off, the weather's turned milder, and I feel great."

Garth took the time to push the rack containing the turkey back into the oven and close the door. He turned and faced her, frowning. "This is the end of November. Winter's just around the corner officially, but up here on this mountain it starts a good month earlier, meaning now. They're already calling for another major snowstorm this weekend. I told you, Kendra, you're safe here, so quit worrying about it. Once you're completely well, and I emphasize the word completely, and the weather has completely broken, and I emphasize the word completely again, we'll plan where you should go and I'll do everything I can to get you someplace you might feel is better. But for now, this place is the safest place in the world for you, damnit."

She studied him a moment, then, without replying, walked into the sunroom, to the windows banking the outer wall. She stood, looking out at the snow-capped mountain peaks.

Garth, feeling remorse for raising his voice, followed her. He stood next to her and stared out at the cloudy afternoon but remained silent.

Kendra studied Garth's reflection in the glass beside her, thinking how handsome he was with his dark-blond hair, blue-green eyes, strong features, and tall, athletic build. She liked how they complemented each other, standing there side by side. She grew surprised at the realization that she was attracted to him.

"I'm sorry I yelled," Garth said.

"I'm glad you care enough to."

They turned toward each other.

"I really love it here. It's so beautiful and peaceful. I'd give anything to stay, I want you to know that."

"So stay."

"I can't, Garth."

"Okay, then, stay longer."

Kendra returned to the window and the beautiful scene before her and seemed to be thinking about this.

Garth forced himself to wait.

She finally turned. "Maybe a little longer."

They smiled at one another, both happy now.

When Thad arrived, he took Kendra into her bedroom, checked her temperature, heart, and pulse, then poked around on her abdomen. He asked questions about how she was feeling, sleeping, eating; liked everything he heard and saw. Afterward, he entered the kitchen ahead of his patient.

"Well?" Garth asked him.

"She's just about completely recovered."

Garth frowned.

"What?"

"She's talking about leaving."

Thad glanced toward the bedroom. "And you don't want her to?"

"Hell, no. Like I told you and her, Thad, for now, this is the safest place for her. You know that."

Thad studied his friend, wondering about his real reason for wanting her to stay. He turned to smile at Kendra as she joined them.

"Well, what's the official verdict? Am I as well as I feel?" she asked Thad.

Thad shrugged. "Kendra, you need to understand, it takes a woman's body a good three months to recover from a miscarriage. You may feel well, but you're still not up to par. Your body's still healing. You need to take it easy the next couple of months, get plenty of rest, give your body a chance to completely recuperate. So, you may feel completely recovered, but you're actually not."

Garth watched Kendra as Thad told her all this. He was mildly surprised to see this news didn't seem to bother her; in fact, she looked a little happy about it.

Thad noticed the same thing and wondered if she actually wanted to continue to stay.

Then Kendra got a suspicious look on her face. "Have you been talking to Garth?"

Garth and Thad glanced at each other.

"About what?" Thad asked.

"About coming up with a reason for me to stay." She frowned at him.

Thad gave her an offended look. "Are you questioning my medical skills?"

Kendra looked chagrined.

"You don't believe me, go see another doctor. He'll tell you the same thing," Thad said, sounding irritated.

Kendra felt terrible. "I'm sorry, Thad. I didn't have the right to say that. Of course, I'm not questioning you."

Thad continued to frown at her. "Then listen to what I have to say here, Kendra. Take the time to let your body heal or your body will never completely heal, not the way it should."

She studied him, wondering what he meant, then the thought fluttered through her mind that maybe she would be endangering her chance of having another child if she didn't follow his instructions and stay healthy. She smiled. "Okay, Thad. Whatever you say. You're the doctor."

Garth and Thad smiled widely.

They had a grand Thanksgiving, the three of them. The lunch Garth prepared, with what little help Kendra and Thad could offer, was delicious and filling. After indulging in the delectable food, they performed the cleanup chores together, then retired to the sunroom for the traditional afternoon of watching football games. Kendra seemed to tire as the day wore on but stayed with them, watching the games, occasionally wandering into the kitchen to snack on Garth's good food, then falling asleep on the couch.

Thad left while she was still sleeping.

Garth walked his friend to the door. "Thanks. I owe you for this."

Thad glanced toward the sunroom. "I really like that girl. I don't want to see anything bad happen to her and my gut feeling is the only person on this earth who can see that it doesn't is you. Don't ask me how I know this, I just do."

Garth nodded. "I feel it, too."

When he entered the sunroom, Kendra was starting to stir, rubbing at her eyes.

"What time is it?" she asked.

"After nine."

"I didn't mean to fall asleep."

"Isn't that what you're supposed to be doing?" Garth teased her.

She smiled at him, then said, "I'm hungry!" and headed for the kitchen.

Garth followed her with a wide grin on his face, realizing how much he enjoyed being with this woman.

Kendra hugged Garth before retiring to her room. "I've never had a Thanksgiving like this. I never knew how wonderful this holiday could be. Thank you for that, Garth."

Garth returned the embrace, then watched her walk away from him, resisting the urge to follow her.

CHAPTER 13

▼

Tony was in a crazed mood Thanksgiving day. He sat in his study, listening to the bustling activity around the mansion, thinking about Angel. If she had been present, she would have given the household staff the day off and they would probably be hosting a catered lunch for people chosen by him; people of power, people who could be manipulated, people who could be utilized. He shifted restlessly, recalling prior conflicts over Thanksgiving. Hell, if he had let her have her way, she'd be down at the mission every damn, friggin' holiday, dishing out food for the homeless. Something he would not allow her to do, not matter how many times she brought it up.

This Thanksgiving, the household staff was not given the day off and all his men were present, on phones or computers, searching the internet, sending and receiving faxes, trying to find his wife.

Tony stood quickly, walked over to the minibar, mixed himself a scotch and soda. He was mildly surprised to find he missed Angel to the extent that he did. But as he told all his mistresses, Tony enjoyed being married. He liked having someone tending to his home; liked having an intelligent, beautiful wife to entertain for him, to show off, even though the façade they presented to the public was not real. He wondered whether she would still love him if she had not found out about her mother; felt hatred toward her father for running his mouth and starting the whole mess. Everything had been perfect to that point. But for twelve years now, his Angel had not given him her love. Tony renewed his vow to himself that one day she would love him, he would see to that. He could do anything if he just put his mind to it.

But look at him now, in a house that felt lonely and empty with no one to share the holiday. Feeling frustrated, out of sorts, Tony threw his glass at the wall. He flung open the door, yelled for Vincent, and instructed him to drive him to the firing range. Nothing was more soothing to Tony than the feel of a hot, smoking gun in his hands.

CHAPTER 14

▼

They were playing Scrabble in front of the fireplace, giving one another a hard time, making up words, challenging each other, trying to prove who was smartest, laughing and having a really good time.

Garth watched Kendra study her letters with a slight frown on her face. Probably trying to formulate a made-up word, Garth thought wryly to himself. He was glad she had decided to stay for awhile, thankful the weather had turned frigid, the roads frozen. Grateful also she was recovering without any sequelae from the miscarriage.

Kendra had begun to join him outdoors and to assist with the daily chores. Although Garth continually told her she didn't need to help, she seemed eager to and told him she enjoyed the work. Both shared a love for horses and took daily rides together. Garth enjoyed showing Kendra the mountain and familiarizing her with the forested area he now considered his home. Although Kendra had never cooked in her life, she found some old cookbooks his mother had used and it seemed daily tackled a different recipe. She was very quickly turning into a good cook, something Garth appreciated. He liked the way she just seemed to fit into his life and was thinking, Why couldn't I have married someone like her? when she glanced up and caught him staring.

As if reading his thoughts, Kendra asked, "What was your wife like?"

Garth blinked in surprise.

She looked embarrassed. "I was just wondering. You don't have to answer. It's no big deal."

"No, it's okay. It's just, I never think about her, to tell you the truth. You kind of caught me off guard." He shrugged. "What was she like?" he asked himself.

"What attracted you to her? Why did you marry her?"

Garth pondered while playing with the wooden squares, rearranging them and placing them back in order. He finally glanced up. "I don't know, to be honest about it. I think we had both reached a point in our lives where we maybe felt we needed someone. We were dating, were attracted to each other." He shrugged. "I don't know. We just seemed to evolve into it, I guess."

She nodded. "What happened then? Why the divorce?"

"Tell you the truth, Keni—" He hesitated when her eyes widened and she stiffened.

"What?" he asked, confused by her reaction.

She smiled at him. "You called me Keni."

Garth contemplated. Did he? He couldn't remember.

"I like it. Keni," she repeated, as if trying out this new name. "Yes, I definitely like that."

Garth nodded, wondering exactly when he had gotten comfortable enough with her to give her a nickname.

She smiled as if reading his thoughts and leaned toward him. "And you were saying?"

He was unsure what she meant and frowned.

"About you and your wife, why you got married, then divorced." She nodded in an encouraging way.

"Oh. Well, let's see." Garth tried to recall what he had been saying. Oh, yeah. "Well, to be honest, I don't think I really loved her and I don't think she really loved me. We were just warm bodies to one another. She was a lawyer and worked long hours. I was always tied up with my work as a police officer. We would see each other maybe one or two nights a week, and even then we'd both be, I don't know, distracted with whatever was going on in our careers at the time. It was not the ideal marriage."

Kendra stared intently at him.

Garth felt uncomfortable. "And then something happened at my job, with my career, that I couldn't handle, and she subsequently couldn't handle me not handling it, so she left. End of marriage. End of story." He gave her a dismissive smile.

He waited for her to ask him the question, but she chose not to.

"What was it like physically? You said you were attracted to her. How were you two physically?"

Garth's brow furrowed, wondering why she would ask that question.

Seeing this, Kendra drew back with a flustered look. "I'm sorry, Garth. It's none of my business. I don't know why I asked you that."

"It's okay. I don't mind. You're talking about sex, I guess. I don't know. It was just sex, just another body there. I don't think we ever really connected in that department. Well, any department, to tell you the truth. It was more a bodily function than an act of love with her." He paused, surprised he had revealed so much to this woman.

Kendra looked down and appeared to be concentrating on her blocks of letters.

"What about Salvatori? How did you come to be with him?"

She leaned back in her chair with a pained expression on her face. "My father owed him a favor. Tony took me as payment."

Garth was surprised. "What?"

"He wanted a wife, and he thought I would do quite nicely."

"Did you love him?"

She shook her head sadly, then glanced at him.

"Yet you married him?"

She nodded.

He thought, She asked me, I'll ask her. "How was it with you two, physically?"

"Terrible," she whispered, her voice shaking, staring at the fire. "I wish I could have at least had that, have known that." She looked at him, her face ashen, tears in her eyes. "I wish more than anything I could know that, but I never will. He made sure of it." She quickly stood, went to her bedroom and closed the door.

Garth stared after her, thinking, I wish I could give that to you, before making himself stop.

CHAPTER 15

▼

James Gallaher, known as Jimmy G. to his friends, all three of them, was having a great Christmas, the best ever. His parents had finally given him the one gift he had longed for, for over a year now, an all-terrain vehicle. After eating a quick breakfast, he was out the door, donning his helmet as he went, calling out to his mom he'd be back by lunch.

Jimmy's family lived in a rural area on the outskirts of North Knoxville consisting of a conglomeration of ridges, just perfect for a four-wheeler. The recent winter storm made it even better, snow and ice to contend with instead of grass and mud. The snow hid rocks and protrusions, making the going dangerous but more fun. Jimmy G. liked to think he was a risk-taker. He would learn before long that he was not.

Jimmy rode his ATV on the paved road long enough to reach one of the higher ridges, right behind the expansive truck stop/restaurant all the truckers seemed to favor. As he climbed the rutted trail snaking over the wooded promontory, a twinkling light kept flashing at his eyes, here one moment, gone the next, as his body shifted with the movements of the four-wheeler. He braked to a stop and glanced around, wondering where the heck that light was coming from. His eyes finally caught a bright glimmer, as of a sunbeam off chrome.

Jimmy climbed further up the ridge, his eyes honing in on the strobing light. He left the furrowed path, traveled about a hundred feet further into the woods, and stopped at a large object covered with brush and bramble. He cut the engine of his ATV, stepped off, and stood studying the scabrous bulk as he took off his helmet. Jimmy slowly approached, wondering what was hidden beneath all this scrub brush and why would anyone bother. He stepped up to it and began pulling limbs and twigs and pine branches away, immediately discerning this was an automobile. He worked slowly, careful not to scratch the surface of the car, just in case it was something he might want. That is, if no one bothered to claim it, he told himself. He finally removed all the detritus on and around the vehicle.

Jimmy stepped back and stared at it a long while, then finally gave a low whistle under his breath. What a friggin' beauty! A sleek Lexus, shimmering in the sun like a shiny black pearl. The windows were darkly tinted, so he leaned closer and tried to peer inside, but couldn't see anything. He put his hand on the handle, and, to his surprise, it lifted and the door swung open easily. Huh! he thought. He stuck his head inside and looked around. Oh, man, this car cost somebody a pretty penny. Leather upholstery, fancy CD player, a bunch of gadgets he couldn't identify. He straightened up and looked around, turning a full 360 degrees. After ascertaining no one was around, he slid onto the driver's seat of the vehicle, being sure to close the door behind him.

Damn! Jimmy thought as he ran his hand over the soft, supple leather. He placed his other hand on the steering wheel, wondering what it'd be like to drive a vehicle such as this. He fantasized all the cute girls who would finally take notice of him if they saw him in something this expensive, not to mention classy.

Curious as to whose car this was and what the heck it was doing here, all covered up, Jimmy opened the glove compartment and rummaged around. He pulled out the vehicle license registration and peered at it in the dim light, finally making out the name Antonio Salvatori. That didn't ring a bell with him, so he placed the registration back and closed the glove compartment. A faint, silverish glint on the floorboard caught his eyes. He reached up, felt around until he found the overhead light, and turned it on. His eyes widened when he realized he was staring at car keys. "Shit!" He picked them up and studied them, trying to ascertain whether he actually had a Lexus key in his hand. Thinking there was no better way to find out than try it, he stuck the key in the ignition, turned it, and laughed gleefully at the sound of a sluggish engine struggling to come to life.

This is too good to be true, Jimmy thought to himself. He turned off the engine, afraid he'd do some damage. If the battery was dying, he didn't want to completely deaden it.

Jimmy sat there a long time, contemplating, then climbed out and walked around the car. He noticed it was mired deeply in snow and mud as he traversed the perimeter of the vehicle, pondering. He came to the conclusion the only reason this car would be here like this was that someone was trying to get rid of it. But who and why? He debated calling this Salvatori guy, but that thought flickered out of his mind quickly when another thought rather rudely intruded. Why not keep it for himself? Get it unstuck, take it to a buddy's dad who owned a questionable garage, see if they couldn't do something about the VIN. Yeah, that's what he'd do. But first he needed to get some battery cables. He could jump it off with his four-wheeler.

Jimmy got busy recovering the car, excited now. Damn, this was the best Christmas ever.

CHAPTER 16

▼

Christmas morning, when Kendra arose, she found Garth in the kitchen, wrestling with a huge ham, preparing it for its doomed trip into the oven. Boo and Sarge watched with interest, ready to charge forward and grab the slab of pork if he dropped it. A large fire crackled in the roomy fireplace and the room smelled of apples and cinnamon intermingled with pine and cedar.

Kendra stood in the doorway watching Garth, marveling at how quickly time had passed since she had been here with him, thinking how much she loved this house and this mountain and, yes, this man. Tears quickly sprang to her eyes at the knowledge that she probably would not be here much longer.

Shaking off her feelings of sadness, Kendra approached Garth and smiled at the grin he gave her when he noticed her.

"Merry Christmas," they said together, then smiled once more.

Garth gave her a teasing look. "I think Santa left something for you last night."

Kendra felt as excited as a child. "Really?" She rushed into the sunroom and looked at the tree they had decorated together, then beneath it. Her eyes widened at what was there.

Kendra turned back to Garth, her eyes glistening with happiness and unshed tears. "The saddle you were working on!" She pulled it from beneath the tree and ran her hands lovingly over the supple leather. She felt movement and glanced up. Garth was standing beside her, watching her.

"I love it, Garth!" She stood and gave him a fierce hug. "I never suspected it was for me." She returned to the saddle and traced the stitchery, admiring his work. "Oh, please, can we go riding this afternoon?" She sounded like a kid again. "I want to try it out, see how it fits."

Garth beamed, thinking this must be what Christmas feels like to the normal folks. He never had liked the holiday much, even when he was married. Hell, even when he was a kid, not with his parents around.

Kendra gave him an impish smile. "I think Santa left something under there for you, too."

Garth gave her a suspicious look.

"I think he hid it behind the tree so you wouldn't see it."

Garth noticed a wrapped box and wondered how in the world he hadn't seen that before. He glanced at Kendra as he pulled it toward him.

Kendra had forgotten about the saddle as she watched Garth. She sat close to him, giving him an excited look. "Go ahead, open it."

Garth tore off the paper and opened the box. His eyes widened at the leather chaps and Western hat nestled in the tissue paper. He looked at her. "This is expensive stuff, Keni. How in the world did you—"

She frowned at him. "It's very rude to question how one finds the means to purchase a gift for someone else."

Garth felt chagrined.

She smiled. "Okay. I had Ted hock my wedding band and engagement ring, and it was just enough to buy this. Isn't it beautiful, Garth? You'll look so handsome in this gear."

"Hey, Keni, you didn't have to do that." He felt terrible she had used so much money on his gift.

She frowned again. "What about the money you could have made off my beautiful saddle?"

"That's different."

She gave him a look.

"What?"

"Are you a sexist? Is that one aspect of your personality I somehow missed?"

Garth couldn't help but grin.

"Say another word about it and I think we're going to have our first fight," Kendra warned.

He recalled the first one, when she had told him she was leaving. "Actually, it would be our second."

"Well, a fight nonetheless."

Garth smiled widely at her, thinking he definitely did not want to fight with her. "Thank you for the gift, Keni. It's beautiful."

"And thank you, Garth." She leaned forward and pecked him on the cheek. She drew back and their eyes met, then their faces moved toward one another. The front door banged open, interrupting them.

"Ho-ho-ho!" Thad yelled. They grinned at one another and rose to greet their friend.

That evening, as they sat side by side on the couch in front of the fire, in companionable silence, enjoying each other's company, drinking wine, Garth felt Kendra staring at him.

He wasn't sure about that look. "What?"

"I just want to thank you, Garth, for giving me the best Christmas ever."

He smiled. "It was fun, wasn't it?"

They had gone riding that afternoon with Thad, appreciating the beautiful, snow-covered scenery, the cold, crisp air, the powerful animals carrying them along. Kendra raved about her beautiful saddle to the point that Garth grew embarrassed, but he was pleased that she loved it. Afterward, they had dinner with their friend, the talk lively and animated and fun, then opened their presents to him and his to them, along with the ones for Boo and Sarge, laughing at the way Boo preferred Sarge's toys to his. Waving Thad off when he left, they performed the cleanup together, feeling almost married, then retired to the sunroom to enjoy the last of the fire before bedtime.

"I've never had a Christmas like this." Kendra sounded wistful. "I finally know what a normal Christmas feels like."

Garth startled a little at that, how she had basically said what he was thinking earlier. "Me either, Keni." He reached over and kissed her cheek. "And I thank you for this day. You've made it special."

"Right back at you," she teased, breaking the moment, moving away before either one did what they really wanted to.

CHAPTER 17

▼

Tony had Vincent drive him to one of his mistress's condominiums. He was in a black mood and wanted some sort of release, hoping sex would accomplish this goal. His Angel had been gone for almost two months now, not one frigging clue as to where she was, and he was almost crazy with anger intermingled with worry. He kept telling himself if something had happened to her, surely he would feel it in his heart. But he didn't. He felt as if she were just fine. "Angel, baby, when I get my hands on you, you won't be walking for a month," he muttered to himself.

Vincent stole a glance at him but didn't say anything as he pulled into the condo's driveway and braked to a stop.

"Stay here." Tony stepped out of the car and went inside.

Rita was waiting on him, giving him a nervous smile as he came through the door. "Merry Christmas, Tony," she said. "I have a gift for you."

Without saying a word, Tony motioned toward the bedroom as he walked that way. She somewhat hastily and anxiously followed him.

Once in the bedroom, Tony began removing his clothes, watching Rita as she did likewise, giving him quick, nervous smiles. She was a beautiful woman, twenty-five, with a perfect body, albeit achieved through artificial means. That bothered him somewhat, comparing her to his Angel, who was all there, nothing added or deleted. He stared at her large, sloping breasts, narrow waist, flat stomach, tapered thighs, and found himself greatly wanting Angel, not this Barbie doll.

Rita finished undressing and reclined on the bed on her side in what he supposed she thought was a seductive pose. This only irritated him more.

Tony pulled over a pillow and placed it on the bed. "Turn over." He waited for her to lay over it, then took her quickly and violently, foregoing any kind of foreplay.

Rita lay beneath him, biting into the bed sheet, trying to keep from crying out, afraid that would excite him more. She was deathly afraid of this man, more so since his wife had left him. He had become uncommunicative and only showed up at her place when he wanted sex or worse. He didn't even talk to her anymore, didn't treat her like a person, just an animal, some means to an end. She had begun thinking maybe it was time to move on to other pastures.

When he was finished, Tony got up and went into the bathroom.

Rita stayed on the bed, unsure what he wanted from her, knowing from past experience, you did not do anything on your own, you let Tony tell you what to do.

Tony returned to the bedroom and began to dress. He watched Rita with a strange look in his eyes.

She tried smiling at him but failed mightily.

Her temerity with him was aggravating. His Angel never would have let him come into her room, motion her toward the bed, done what he told her to do, taken her with such force, without some kind of response, shown some kind of independence, some backbone. This woman was nothing but a piece of meat and Tony felt contempt for her.

"You want me to get dressed, Tony?" Rita's hand idly rubbed her upper thigh as she tried to look sexy, which he thought only looked pathetic.

"Get up."

Rita quickly stood and approached him, walking with an exaggerated sway that made him angry. His Angel never walked like that, like some common slut.

"Bend over." Tony pointed at the bed, then shot his cuffs.

Rita gave him a questioning look before complying, raising her buttocks seductively.

Tony caressed her bare skin, his hands sliding over each firmly exercised cheek, watching her arch her back with a passion he felt to be artifice. He stepped back, shucked the belt out of his pants, and made her pay for what she was.

Vincent heard the screams from outside but didn't move.

"Merry Christmas," Tony muttered as he left the bedroom. He stepped out of the condo, buckling his belt, and got into the car. His eyes met Vincent's in the rear-view mirror. "Take me home, then come back and take care of this."

Without saying a word, Vincent did as told.

CHAPTER 18

▼

They were putting the finishing touches on what Garth thought of as a great day. He and Kendra had done chores together in the morning, then gone for a long ride. They spent the afternoon in the sunroom, working on their own projects. Garth was restoring an old saddle that had been molding for years in one of his neighbor's barns and Kendra had begun a quilt, her first. Early evening, they fixed dinner together, then shared cleanup.

Garth was distractedly thinking this felt like a marriage, a very comfortable, companionable, albeit sans intimacy marriage, when Kendra spoke up after a long silence.

"I'm leaving tomorrow."

Garth took the time to put down the plate he was holding before he turned to her.

Kendra glanced at him, then away, to the sink. She pulled the drain and watched the gray water swirl toward the opening.

Garth waited.

Kendra busied herself folding the dishcloth. "You've been so great, Garth, but I can't stay here anymore. It's, well, it's just too dangerous."

Garth felt betrayed by her words. "I'll protect you," he said in a harsh voice.

She turned to him and there were tears in her eyes. "No, no, that's not what I'm saying. I'm not worried about my safety. I'm worried about yours, what he'll do to you if he finds me here with you."

"I'm a big boy, I can take care of myself." Garth watched one lone tear travel down her cheek. She didn't wipe it away.

"I care about you, Garth," Kendra whispered. "Greatly. And I could not live with myself if he hurt you or, God forbid, killed you. Please understand. I'd rather go back to him, live with him, be his wife, than let that happen to you."

"You don't know that he's ever going to track you here." Garth tried to keep the desperate tone out of his voice.

"He will. It's only a matter of time."

"So you go where?" His voice turned bitter. "On to some other person's house, some other city, some other state? Live off the land? Go to a homeless shelter? What the hell are you planning on doing, Kendra?"

Her eyes plead with him. "I'll be fine. I'll go where I go, that's all. God took care of me before by sending me to you, he will now."

Garth gave her a stubborn look. "I can take care of you."

"At the cost of your own life, and I will not have that!" She was crying openly. "You mean the world to me, Garth, and I will not let him take that away from me. Not this time. If it means living in poverty or imprisonment the rest of my life, I will gladly accept that. Don't you understand?"

"But I can protect you. I'm your best chance," Garth said, raising his voice.

"No. The price is too heavy, and I won't let you do that." Kendra wiped at her tears. "I'm leaving tomorrow, Garth. That's it. I've made up my mind."

Kendra walked away, then turned back to him. "I want to thank you for saving my life, taking me in, helping me, doing all you've done for me. I'm sorry I've put so much on you. I'll find a way some day to repay you, I promise."

"I don't need any kind of payment from you!" Garth yelled at her.

Kendra turned and left. Garth heard her gently close her bedroom door.

"Shit!" he yelled, throwing the dishtowel in the sink. He picked it up and began hitting it against the cabinet, yelling, "Shit" over and over again.

Finally, breathing heavily, he leaned over the sink, thinking. He caught movement in his peripheral vision and looked that way. Boo and Sarge were watching him. "I can't let her leave," he said to them. He straightened up and walked to her bedroom. The two animals followed solemnly behind.

Garth didn't knock on her door this time.

Kendra was packing her few clothes into a backpack he had given her. She glanced at him when he opened the door, then resumed what she had been doing.

Garth watched her for a moment before stepping into the bedroom. "Okay," he said, trying to make his voice calm, trying to be reasonable. "You don't feel safe here, fine. That's fine. We'll leave."

She stopped her movements and frowned at him.

"I'm not going to live the rest of my life, Kendra, wondering, worrying every damn minute of every damn day where the hell you are, what the hell you're doing, and whether or not he has found you, and if so, what he's done to you." Garth's voice rose angrily.

"You don't want to stay here, you want to leave, fine, but I'm going with you. I care about you, too, in case you haven't figured that out yet. And I will not, and I repeat, will not, let that man get to you, Kendra, if it's the last thing I do."

She burst into tears. "But don't you understand? That probably will be the last thing you do. Garth, he's violent, he's vindictive. He doesn't have a conscience at all. He feels no remorse, nothing except this great need to tame me. You will mean nothing to him and he will kill you with no thought about it at all. Please, I couldn't live with that. Please don't make me live with that." She sat down on the bed, sobbing now, and put her hands over her face.

Garth waited for her to calm. "It is my choice, Kendra, what I do with my life. And my choice is to be with you, to help you, protect you, take care of you. You've become my best friend, and I could not live with myself, knowing I let you go when I could have helped you. So I will leave with you tomorrow and we'll go wherever you feel you need to go. But you won't leave by yourself."

She looked at him. Tears were falling silently now. "But what about Boo and Sarge and the horses and this beautiful place, Garth? This is your haven. And it's been mine, too. How can you leave this? What will happen to the animals?"

"Thad can take care of them until we get back. And yes, it was my haven, after you came. It won't be when you leave."

Garth walked toward the door, then turned back. "And don't think you're going to sneak out tonight, Kendra, behind my back. Because if you do that, then you'll have two of us after you, and I think I'm the better tracker."

Kendra turned away from him.

He quietly closed the door.

That night, Garth kept the hall light on and his bedroom door open, keeping vigil, afraid in his heart Kendra would sneak out and get away and be gone from his life. He didn't think he could live with that. He had known for awhile now that this was the woman he wanted to spend the rest of his life with. And if it meant having a shorter life span, well, then, so be it. He would not give her up. He could not.

He heard her door snick open, then a rustling in the hallway, saw her shadow on the wall before she actually appeared in his doorway. Boo, who was lying on the floor at the foot of Garth's bed, raised his head and began whining. Garth ignored him, watching beneath slitted eyes as Kendra stood uncertainly in the threshold. He waited to see what she would do.

She finally stepped into the room. He immediately felt relief.

"Garth," Kendra said, her voice barely audible.

He kept still. "Yeah."

She walked closer.

He raised up on his elbows, watching her.

She hesitated at the foot of the bed. "I've been thinking about what we talked about before." She looked down at her hands, which he noticed she was wringing nervously.

He remained silent.

She sighed, then looked at him. "You're my best friend, too, and I don't want to lose you either." Her voice cracked, and she took a minute, breathing deeply. "If you insist on endangering your own life for my sake, I can't stop you, although I wish I could, because I know if you lost your life because of me, I could not live with myself. But you're bigger than I am, you're stronger than I am." She glanced at him and he caught the faint trace of a wistful smile. "So, if you won't let me leave without you, then I won't let you leave this beautiful place. I'll stay if that's what will keep you here. I'll take my chances, but I want you to understand that if he shows up here and anything happens to you, it happens to me. I won't live without you."

Her words were intense and he could feel her stare without seeing it.

He sat up. "Come here, Keni."

She approached the side of the bed and sat down.

He took her hands in his own. "I'm sorry I got so rough with you."

"You didn't." She gave him a quick smile. "More like intensely passionate."

"Believe it or not, Keni, this is the best, safest place for you. We're almost isolated here. It's not an easily accessible place and he'll have to work hard to get up this mountain if he ever does track you here. But we can make it harder on him."

"What do you mean?"

"I know this mountain like the back of my hand. We can set up safe places, hidey-holes for weapons, alarms to let us know if anyone's close, that sort of thing. We can work out a plan of action if he ever does show himself."

She studied him. "You think it could work?"

He could detect the hope in her voice. "We'll make it work," he said, his voice more confident than he felt.

She hugged him. "I meant what I said before," she whispered against his neck.

"What was that?"

"About God leading me to you. I really, truly believe that."

"That's a beautiful thought, Keni," he said, his lips against her hair.

Kendra drew back from him. "Tell me what we need to do."

Garth stretched out on the bed, and she lay beside him, holding his hand.

They fell asleep planning. Sometime during the night, Kendra rolled against him, placing one arm over him, snuggling her head into his shoulder. Garth put his arms around her and held her protectively before falling back to sleep. And that night, for the first time in a very long time, he did not dream the dream.

CHAPTER 19

▼

The next morning, Garth showed Kendra the gun safe. He encouraged her to handle the different weapons resting inside in order to gauge which ones felt comfortable in her hands. Seeing the vast amount of weaponry, she gave him a questioning look.

"My dad was a collector. The only guns I own I used when I was a cop. I'm not what you might consider a fancier."

Kendra's brow was furrowed. "I always hated those things." Without explaining, Garth knew it probably came from her association with her husband.

She was tentative at first, but he had her lift each firearm and hold it to determine which ones she felt most comfortable with. She finally chose a mini Glock .40 and Colt and Wesson .380 semi-automatic.

Garth spent the afternoon showing Kendra how to break them down, clean them, put them back together, load, unload, engage the safety, disengage it. He had her repeat this until she could practically do it blindfolded.

The next day, Garth set up a target area made out of bales of hay on which he spray-painted a man's torso. He showed Kendra the proper stance, which part of the body to aim at for the kill, then had her practice shooting at the target for over an hour.

In a very short while, Kendra grew comfortable and began showing some expertise at handling a firearm. They devoted at least an hour each day to target practice, and her skills seemed to improve with each outing. Garth was impressed with her ability to handle such a deadly weapon.

"I probably come by it honest. My father loved guns." She hesitated. "I was hoping he hadn't passed on any of his qualities to me."

"This might not be such a bad quality to have, considering the circumstances," Garth observed.

Their days were spent exploring the mountainside, discovering safe places, planning alternate routes of escape, planting weapons here and there, leaving sites arranged in such a way that would tell them someone had trespassed when they checked.

Garth taught Kendra how to use a knife, how to fight with one, and where to hide it. Kendra likewise adapted to this rather quickly. "Call it survival instinct," she said when he questioned this.

Garth held a black belt in karate and decided it wouldn't hurt to teach Kendra a few things so she could protect herself if the need arose. They were in the yard, and Garth patiently held forth on the advantages of knowing karate, went into a little of its history, and began to show Kendra the proper stance, the right way to hold her hands. She went along willingly enough.

Garth stepped back from her. "Okay, come at me like you're going to attack me, and I'll show you what you can do to deflect an attack."

Kendra immediately began moving around Garth, yelling, "Whock, whock, whock," giving imitation karate chops, slicing the air, occasionally giving out an aiiieee yell, then "Whock, whock, whock," slashing at the air while dancing around him.

Garth folded his arms and waited her out.

She postured like a vulture, imitating the stance of the Karate Kid, then whirled around him again, with the whock, whock, whocks.

Garth was growing irritated.

Kendra drew closer, and when she came within range, Garth swept her feet out from under her. She landed on her butt.

"Ow!" she yelled, falling back, "that hurt."

Garth leaned over her and glared into her face. "I'm serious here."

Kendra grinned up at him. "You didn't take me seriously?"

Garth gave her a stern look. "I know you weren't serious."

Kendra sighed. "Okay. Just help me up, I'll get serious." She extended one arm.

Garth reached down, grabbed her arm, helped her up, and before he knew it, she had flipped him and he was on the ground on his back.

He gritted his teeth against saying, "Ow."

Kendra leaned over him and looked him in the face. "That serious enough for you?"

"I take it you know karate."

She sat down beside him. "A little. Vinnie taught me some of the martial arts." She smiled at him.

Garth raised up on his elbows. "Who's Vinnie?"

"Tony's personal bodyguard, the guy who drives him around, his right-hand man, so to speak, but the only one in Tony's camp who actually paid me any mind."

"Yeah?" Garth was interested. Kendra didn't usually talk about her life with Tony.

"Vinnie's an expert at martial arts. He knew it interested me, and the times when Tony was away and Vinnie wasn't with him, he'd teach me karate."

Garth sat up and crossed his legs.

She caught him looking. "What?"

He cocked his head, smiling. "It's just, you're such a normal person, Keni. Well, maybe not normal, you're too wacky for that."

She grinned with pleasure at this.

"I don't know how you could have endured all you did and ended up as normal as you are."

Kendra shrugged her shoulders.

Garth waited.

She looked away from him.

"How'd you stand it, living like that?" he asked her, his voice gentle.

She began plucking at the grass. "I was a psychology major. I learned how to be normal."

"How'd you stand it, Keni, living like that, with him?"

After she had plucked a few more grass blades, Kendra glanced at him, then back down to the grass. "Actually, I never knew anything else. My dad was a strict authoritarian, and if I dared defy him, I paid for it, in the physical sense. Tony was the same way. Maybe I expected it, I don't know. But one thing I did know with Tony was if I ever allowed him to control me, to dominate me, then it would be over for me. Therein lay his passion for me, the need to control someone who would not be controlled."

"And got the shit beat out of you for it."

She shrugged. "Call it survivor instinct, but I knew that if I became subjugated to him, he would tire of me fairly quickly. But Tony would never let me go, not his wife. I probably would have met up with an unfortunate accident or something." She looked at him and the pain in her eyes was horrible for him.

"You really believed that?"

"I knew that."

"Ah, Keni."

Her eyes shimmered with nascent tears.

"I promise you, you will never have to endure anything like that again," Garth said, his voice almost a whisper.

"No, don't." She placed her fingers on his lips.

He took her hand in his and kissed her fingers. "I will protect you."

She stared at him a long time. "Maybe, with God's help." She sighed. "If anyone can, Garth, I think you're the only one who could." She stood and went into the house.

An hour each day was devoted to karate and sparring with one another. They had a lot of fun with this aspect of what Kendra had come to term her "survival training." She would usually end up on the ground, holding her stomach, laughing to the point of crying, Garth standing over her, giving her exasperated looks. But he was glad to hear her laugh, see her take enjoyment from life, which he rightly suspected had not been part of her existence before.

Evenings were quiet. They would lie on the couch, Garth at one end, Kendra at the other, exhausted from their training during the day, either quietly watching TV or reading. More than once, they would fall asleep there, and Garth would come awake during the night to find Kendra had crawled up to lie beside him, on her side, her back against the couch, her head on his shoulder, her arm over his body. It bothered yet touched him that she would trust herself to be intimate with him only when he was asleep. He wouldn't wake her, though, choosing to stay there, wrapping his arms around her, holding her body to his, wondering if they were ever going to consummate what they both knew was happening between them. He would fall back to sleep and never dreamed the dream when Kendra was with him.

CHAPTER 20

▼

Dana Staples was young, beautiful, and happy. Her recent move to Miami, Florida had been a good one. Although she aspired to be a model, her height interfered. She had a face she knew was more than pretty and which the camera seemed to enhance. Her coloring was good. Her dark-gray eyes framed with sooty lashes were her most alluring feature. She knew she should be in better shape and had joined a gym. It wouldn't take long to achieve the body she wanted, her trainer had told her. She had just signed with an agency, was assured she would be given work as an actress, and, in fact, had an audition for a commercial the next day.

Dana picked up the phone, called her parents in Memphis, and told them the great news, knowing how they worried about her, feared for her safety away from them. She told them life was beautiful, couldn't be better. Her feeling was infectious. They were happy for her, excited by her news.

Dana did not know that she had less than twenty-four hours to live.

Dana's parents, who loved their daughter deeply and had made her their number-one priority in their lives, did not know that their darkest nightmare would soon be realized and that they would, within the next seventy-two hours, be claiming the body of their only child, who would only be identified through dental records.

CHAPTER 21

▼

They had fallen asleep on the couch watching a DVD of Kendra's favorite movie, "The Last of the Mohicans." Garth came awake, feeling Kendra shift in his arms. He glanced at her, thinking she must have just now lain beside him, and was surprised to see she was staring at him.

He rubbed his eyes. "Thought you were asleep."

"What do you dream about?" she asked in a low voice. "Who's your demon, Garth?"

"It's nothing, Keni." He made as if to get up. "Come on, we better get to bed. It's late."

She remained where she was and her weight kept his arm pinned beneath her back.

Garth stared at her.

She gave him a curious look. "You know my demon. Why won't you tell me about yours?"

He didn't answer.

"You don't seem to have the bad dreams when we fall asleep together."

"Oh, you noticed that, huh?" he asked, trying to make his voice sarcastic.

"What happened, Garth? What do you keep reliving? What's haunting you?"

"Later." He tried to rise once more.

"No, now," she said in a firm voice. "You can tell me, don't you know that? You can share anything with me."

He stared at her a long moment, once more appreciating her beauty, her sereneness, the calming effect she had on him.

She waited patiently.

He lay back down.

She continued to watch him.

He looked away from her. "I was a hostage negotiator, but you know that. This happened during a bank robbery. This young dude, out of his mind on some kind of hallucinogen, goes into this bank, carrying a semiautomatic, goes through the door, starts shooting up the place. I mean, that bank was an abattoir by the time he got through. And he kills everybody in there but this one woman."

He glanced at Kendra, then away. "She had your eyes, Keni. Beautiful eyes."

He stopped, remembering. After awhile, he began again. "And she was pregnant. Very pregnant. After he has her collect all the money for him, he decides he's going to use her as a hostage, get away using her."

Kendra made a moaning sound deep in her throat, as of a wounded animal.

Garth felt the hairs on the back of his neck rise in response. "KPD had him cornered there in the bank, no way out, and I got there maybe ten minutes after he took her. He was at the front door, yelling, her in front of him, the gun pointed at her head, demanding safe passage or he'd kill her." He shook his head. "I broke protocol, went right up to the bastard, offered myself instead of her, tried to talk him into releasing her, taking me instead." His voice cracked. He was breathing heavily and beads of sweat puddled on his upper lip and forehead.

Kendra picked up his hand and kissed his palm, then placed her own in his, before turning back to him.

"He killed her," Garth said in a pained voice. "Took the frigging gun, right as I reached for her, and put it against the side of her head and blew her away."

Kendra put her hand on his face and made soothing noises in her throat.

"You know what I remember?" Garth glanced at her, then away. "Those big, beautiful, gray eyes of her, pleading with me, asking me not to let him hurt her, not to let him kill her. And what did I do? The stupidest thing in the world; approached him out in the open, offering myself, when I should have known that's exactly what he would do."

Kendra stroked his arm. "You were only trying to save her, Garth."

"I killed her," he said, his voice pressured. "It's my fault she died. She asked for my protection and I killed her."

"No, no," Kendra said in an urgent voice. "Oh, Garth, honey, no. Not you. He would have killed her anyway, you know that." She put her hand against his cheek and turned his face to her. "You know that," she said, her voice hard.

He didn't answer her.

"What'd you do to him?"

"Killed the son of a bitch. Grabbed that semi out of his hands, blew that psycho off the face of this Earth."

Kendra nodded. "Good for you. You avenged her, Garth. Good for you."

"No, I killed her," he said, almost choking on the words.

Kendra raised up. "You did what you could for her, Garth. I'm sure she knew that. At least when she died, she had you with her. She wasn't alone with some crazy homicidal idiot. At least the last thing she saw was you."

Garth remained silent.

Kendra sat on her knees. "I owe her. I owe her in a huge way."

Garth was confused. "Owe her? For what, Keni? You didn't even know her."

She leaned closer, her voice barely a whisper. "If that hadn't happened, if she had lived, you wouldn't have quit KPD, you wouldn't have come to this place, you wouldn't have been living here when I got here, Garth, and you wouldn't have saved my life."

He shifted restlessly.

"No, don't deny it. You saved my life. She may not have lived, but in her dying, she saved me through you. Don't you see that? I would have died in your barn that night if you hadn't found me. You know that. I've heard Thad say the same thing. And whether you want to believe it or not, Garth, God sent me here. I know he did. You were meant to save me, and you have, and I'll owe you forever. And her, that poor woman, I owe her, too. I just hope it will be enough for you knowing that you at least saved me."

Garth sat up. "No, Keni. I didn't save you, but I thank God I found you."

"You saved me. And I'm not speaking physically, Garth. You saved my soul, too. You have to know that. I was dead inside, before you."

They sat, face to face, gazing at one another, silent. He wanted her badly, could sense she felt the same, and just as he reached for her, she abruptly left the couch, escaped to her room, and closed the door behind her.

CHAPTER 22

▼

Tony insisted every possible lead to his Angel's whereabouts be investigated, and this kept Vincent and Tony's minions busy because it seemed everyone, in their great quest to curry Tony's favor, saw Angel at every corner.

Vincent sat in Tony's office, updating him on the latest concerning his missing wife, which was nothing but a bunch of false leads that had been checked and rechecked.

Mark, who aspired to become closer to Tony, maybe his left-hand man since Vinnie still seemed to be held in high regard by their boss, even after his major screw-up, burst into the office, waving a faxed picture in the air. "I think we got her." Mark looked both excited and pleased with himself.

Vincent gave Mark an exasperated look, aggravated at his audacity to come into the boss's office without so much as a knock. He made a mental note to make sure Mark understood he had just broken one major rule, if Tony didn't first.

Tony, though, seeing the look on Mark's face, waved him over, grabbed the faxed sheet out of his hand, and studied it.

"Where?" He glanced at Mark as he handed Vincent the picture.

Vincent studied it closely, wondering how the hell you could tell anything for sure from a grainy fax.

"Miami, Florida," Mark said.

"They sure it's her?" Vincent asked him.

Mark shrugged. "All they told me was this girl could be her twin if it's not her."

"They give you a name?" Vincent asked.

"Yeah, but it's not Angel Salvatori." Mark drew the fax away and glanced at his notes on the back. "Girl goes by the name of Dana Staples. Moved there just recently from Memphis, so she told her super. Chestnut-colored hair, gray eyes, five-seven, about 120 pounds."

Vincent looked at Tony, who nodded.

"You want they should investigate further?" Mark eagerly looked back and forth between the two.

Tony thought a minute. "Nah. We'll handle it ourselves." He turned to Vincent. "Get packed. We leave in an hour." He glanced at Mark. "You, too, you're going with us."

Mark tried to suppress his look of triumph.

Vincent rose from the chair. "We driving or flying?"

"We'll take the plane. Call our pilot, tell him to make the arrangements."

Tony turned to Mark and motioned toward the fax. "Call these people. Tell them, keep an eye on her. She tries to leave, hold her for us."

"No problem." Mark snatched up the picture and left.

Vincent stayed behind.

Tony looked at him. "What?"

"Chances are it might not be her. You can't tell from a faxed photo."

Tony shrugged dismissively. "Maybe. But I gotta do something here. I'm going out of my mind. And if it's not Angel, she'll do."

Vincent gave him a sharp look, but Tony motioned for him to leave.

They arrived in Miami around noon. After checking into the exclusive hotel Tony frequented when he visited that city, Mark called the investigator who had faxed him the photo. He was told where the girl lived and that she hadn't left there all day.

Tony thought a minute. "All right, this is what we're gonna do. Vinnie, you find me a place I can rent. I don't care how much it costs, but I want it isolated, not like a condo or hotel room. Away from everything, and I mean everything, you understand?"

Vincent nodded, his face neutral.

Tony turned his attention to Mark, who was eager and ready. "You camp out at her place. She leaves, you follow her. I want you to call me every hour on the hour and let me know where she is. You got that?"

"Yeah, boss. I'm on my way."

Tony glanced at Vincent and caught his look. "You got something you want to say?"

Vincent thought a moment. "Nope." He picked up the phone.

The realtor Vincent contacted quickly located a house on the ocean with its own private beach, which she repeatedly assured him was isolated, nothing but empty sand for miles around. Even though Tony only wanted it for one day, they had to pay a month's rent of ten thousand dollars.

Tony didn't object, saying, "Rent it."

After Vincent rented a luxury car, he met with the realtor to exchange a check for keys and directions, then drove Tony to the beach house. Tony walked through the rooms, checking it out, then had Vincent drive around the area, ascertaining it was as isolated as the realtor claimed. Once he was satisfied, Tony picked up his cell phone, dialed Mark, and asked where she was.

"Since she walked her dog a couple of hours ago, she ain't come back out." Mark was enjoying this surveillance work.

"You get a good look at her face?" Tony asked. "You know if it's her or not?"

Mark paused while considering how to respond. He had been Angel's body-guard and had watched her enough to know the way she moved. Even though he had seen this woman only from a distance, he was beginning to think this wasn't Tony's wife. He wondered what would happen if he had led his boss on a wild-goose chase. He didn't want to think about that, remembering what had happened to that trooper. "I can't tell. I haven't been able to get close enough to her."

Tony turned to Vincent. "Take me back to the beach house, go get Mark, grab her, and bring her to me." He spoke into the phone again. "Vinnie's coming to get you." He terminated the call.

Vincent didn't like this. "What if it's not Angel?"

"Bring her anyway," Tony said, his eyes darkening, ignoring his driver's questioning look.

It was dark by the time Vincent reached where Mark had set up surveillance.

Mark trotted over to the car, opened the door, and dropped into the passenger sear.

"She still there?"

"Yep. Lucky for me, she's had her blinds open all day, so I can see her go back and forth. She just passed by a minute ago."

They debated how they could get her into the car. Dana helped solve the problem by stepping out of the front entrance with her dog on a leash, going for a walk.

Vincent fell in behind her and drove at a slow pace. They waited until she had gone into an area darkened by trees with foliage thick enough to block light thrown from the streetlights. Mark lunged out of the car and grabbed her, placing his hand over her mouth as he yanked the dog's leash out of her hand. He threw her in the back seat before she could get a scream out, using his body to block her exit from the car. He quickly closed the door and Vincent engaged the locks in the back. After Mark had joined him up front, they sped away.

"What are you doing?" Dana screamed at them, yanking on the door handle. "Let me out!" She pulled on the knob, trying to unlock the door.

They remained silent, watching her.

Vincent finally glanced at Mark.

Mark looked sick. "It's not her."

"I know."

"What are we gonna do?"

"Tony wants her anyway." Vincent drove on, trying to ignore the young woman screaming in the back.

By the time they arrived at the beach house, Dana was silently crying. After her initial hysterics, she had asked them repeatedly why they were doing this to her, please couldn't they just let her go, please not to hurt her, please, please, please. Vincent had fought the urge to jab her in the mouth to shut her up.

Vincent braked to a stop in front of the beach house. Mark hopped out, waited for Vincent to disengage the locks, then opened the back door and pulled their hostage out of the car.

Dana didn't struggle or try to run away, just stood passively looking up at the beach house. "Why have you brought me here?" she asked in a pitiful voice.

"Somebody wants to see you." Vincent nodded at Mark to take her inside.

Tony was in the living room, staring out at the foaming ocean, when Mark led the young woman into the room. Tony walked closer to study her. She had Angel's hair color, yet her hair was longer and coarser, and cut in a different style. Her face was sharper, her body slightly heavier through the breasts and hips. She was probably five years younger, her features not as mature as his precious wife's. She had a light sprinkling of freckles across her nose, which she had tried to cover with makeup. Tony supposed, from a distance, she would be the spitting image. "Well, they were right about one thing. She could be my Angel's twin," he observed. Still gazing at Dana, he told Mark to leave.

Mark left in a hurry, glad to get away from his boss.

Vincent entered the room. "It's not her, Tony. Let me take her back."

Tony looked at him with surprise; Vinnie usually followed orders and kept his mouth shut.

Tony put his hand under Dana's chin, lifted her head, stared into her eyes. "I got plans for this girl."

A soft whimper issued from Dana's mouth.

"She's not Angel," Vincent repeated.

"She's not Angel, but she'll do," Tony said, his voice soft. "She'll do quite nicely."

"Please." Dana looked beseechingly at Vincent. "I haven't done anything. I don't know who you people are. Please, let me go. I won't tell anyone." This last statement turned into a wail.

Vincent tried again. "It's not her, Tony. You can see that. She has nothing to do with this."

Tony turned on him. His eyes were dark and glittering, as evil as a demon's.

Vincent stiffened.

"Wait outside with Mark. I'll let you know when I need you," Tony snapped.

Vincent looked from the crying woman to Tony, then away.

"You got something you want to say to me?" Tony yelled.

This startled Dana, who began to wail louder.

Vincent turned and left.

Tony waited until Vincent was gone, then turned his attention to the woman.

"Please, mister, please. I haven't done anything. Please let me go."

Tony smiled benignly at her, giving her a glimmer of hope. "First, we're gonna have a little welcome back," he said, his hand traveling to his belt.

Dana's eyes widened with horror as she watched Tony unbuckle his belt, then unfasten his pants.

Tony advanced toward her. "And afterward, we're gonna discuss you running off like you did, Angel."

"But I'm not Angel!" she yelled as loudly as she could. "My name's Dana. Dana Staples. I'm not your Angel."

Tony grabbed her, pulled her to the lounge, and threw her down. "Maybe not, but you'll do just fine."

Vincent stood outside with Mark, smoking a cigarette, waiting. At first they heard Tony's muffled voice, the woman's protesting responses. However, before long, she began to shriek loudly.

Mark gave Vincent a sick look. "What's he doing to her?"

Vincent shook his head at him with disgust. "I think you know what he's doing to her." He threw down the cigarette he had been smoking and pulled out another one. He had heard Tony rape a woman enough times to know what the shrieks meant.

"But it's not Angel. What's he want with her?"

"She may not be Angel, but for now, to Tony, she is."

Mark gave Vincent a wild look. "He's crazy. You know that, man. He's out of control. Why don't you do something? Why don't you stop him?"

Vincent glared at Mark. "You think he ought to be stopped? Go stop him."

Mark knew better. "Oh, shit, why did I ever have to show him that picture?" Mark moaned, as Dana's shrieks seemed to reach a crescendo, then die.

They could hear moaning sounds coming from the young woman inside.

Vincent threw down his cigarette and brought his face close to Mark's. "Whatever happens to her, you did, you just remember that. You should have investigated this one further before taking it to him, you damn, stupid fool."

Mark covered his ears when she began shrieking again, but Vincent pulled them away, forcing him to listen as Tony violated Dana, then began beating her. They could hear the muffled sounds as he pummeled her skin with whatever he chose to use on her, her piercing screams, which seemed to fade quickly.

Vincent forced himself to remain where he was, resisting the urge to go inside and stop Tony. He knew the only way he could do that would be to kill him, but this was not the time for that. Too many of Tony's people knew where he was, his reason for being in Miami. There would be too much explaining to do and not enough time to cover his tracks.

Mark threw up as the beating continued, but Vincent felt no sympathy for him. He stood there, hating that man inside, glad it wasn't Angel who was having to endure what her surrogate was, thinking, If he does that to her when he finds her, I'll kill him.

Long after the girl had stopped making any sound at all, the beating continued.

Mark began dry heaving, mumbling, "Oh, God," and "Oh, shit," continuously, acting agitated.

Vincent slapped him in the face, hard.

Mark looked at him, his eyes crazed.

"He's gonna come out here any minute now and expect us to go in there and clean up his mess. And you're gonna do the cleanup, because you brought this on. This is your doing, you stupid prick. But let me tell you something first. Tony sees you out here throwing up, he sees you standing around wringing your hands, acting all upset, hears you whining about what have you done, he's gonna do the same thing to you he did to her, only longer. Now, get your ass under control before he sees you."

Mark gulped loudly several times and began breathing heavily. "He's killed her," he said, his voice cracking. "I just know he's killed her."

"And you're responsible for that," Vincent spat at him. "Now, straighten up your ass and get ready for what's coming."

After what seemed an eternity, Tony finally opened the door. His clothing was covered with blood and his eyes held a gleeful cast. He looked at Vinnie. "I'm gonna take a shower. Get that mess in there cleaned up before I come down again." He left the door open and went upstairs.

"Oh, shit," Mark muttered as they entered the house.

The smell of blood was heavy in the air, the room where the body lay saturated with it. Dana Staples, twin to Angel Salvatori, was on the floor, a pulpous mesh of flesh and blood and bone and cartilage.

Mark took one look, then ran outside, dry heaving. Vincent went and got him.

CHAPTER 23

▼

Jimmy was back at the Lexus, where he had been spending a lot of time lately, either sitting in the car daydreaming or working around it. He had begun placing twigs and foliage in front of and behind the tires, preparing the ground for when it would be dry enough to try to drive the car out of the hole in which it was mired.

He had jumper cables with him which he had taken from his mom's trunk, hoping she wouldn't notice them missing and question him about where they could be, and was attaching them from the battery of his ATV to the battery of the Lexus. He kept telling himself positive to positive, negative to negative, praying he was doing it right, knowing the danger if he wasn't.

Jimmy stepped back after completing this task and went over the procedure in his mind, remembering what his dad had always told him, making sure the batteries were connected in the right way. Feeling confident he hadn't made any mistakes, he opened the door to the Lexus, settled into the driver's seat, fished the key out of his jeans pocket, and inserted it into the ignition. He mumbled, "Please, start; please, start," as he turned the key. The Lexus gave a grudging grind, and he frowned, turned the key back, and started all over again, beginning with his mantra. This time, he smiled widely when the engine caught and bellowed. Remembering he had his foot stomped on the accelerator and could flood it if he wasn't careful, he removed his foot and sat back, listening happily to the sound of a smoothly running engine. "All right!" he sang.

Jimmy climbed out of the car to disconnect the cables, but left it running so that the battery would charge. He made sure to pack the jumpers away in his four-wheeler, telling himself he better not forget to put those back in his mom's trunk like tonight. He stood, heeding the car's engine.

He walked around, checking the ground, wondering if it was dry enough to try to move the car out of its rut. What the heck, he'd give it a try. If it wouldn't budge, he'd quit. He wouldn't dig it in any deeper. Jimmy got back in the car, put the gear shift into drive, released the emergency brake, put his foot on the accelerator, and barely gave the car gas. He felt it ease forward a little before settling back into the rut.

Damn! he thought, then decided he'd try it in reverse. He put the gearshift into the reverse position and slowly eased his foot down on the gas pedal. He felt the car begin to go backwards, then stop. He heard the wheels spinning and cursed. He let the car settle back into the rut, telling himself he needed to be patient, give it more time. The days were growing warmer; it wouldn't be long now.

CHAPTER 24

▼

After their daily patrol on horseback, Garth led Kendra to a small meadow near the cabin. The prior summer, he had dammed the stream that meandered through the clearing enough to create a small swimming hole for the hot weather. They stood on a large, flat rock he utilized as a diving board above the deepest part, admiring the cool-blue pond.

Kendra was delighted with Garth's surprise and bemoaned the fact that the water was too cold for swimming.

Garth smiled at her, proud of her reaction. "It'll be warm enough in another month, I guess."

Kendra leaned forward and peered into the water. "What's that, Garth?"

He stared but couldn't see anything. "What?"

"Out in the water. Don't you see it?"

He shook his head, casting his eyes across the clear, gurgling water.

She moved behind him and pointed with her arm around him. "There—oh, did you see it? There, Garth, look." She sounded excited.

"Look at what?" He walked to the edge of the rock and studied the water.

"Bend over a little, you can see it better," she said from behind him.

Without thinking, Garth did, and before he knew it, Kendra had pushed him in. He came up sputtering.

She was doubled over, laughing.

"It's freezing in here!" Garth roared.

Kendra pointed at him. "You should have known," she said, as if to absolve responsibility for her behavior.

Garth came out of the water, violently shaking, making his teeth jitter, in essence, dramatically acting as if he were freezing to death.

Kendra immediately stopped laughing and looked at him with concern. "Oh, my gosh, Garth, I didn't know it would be that cold." She ran over to him. "Oh, I'm so sorry. Here, let's get you back home…" She squealed when he picked her up in his arms and kicked her feet, protesting, as he walked onto the rock and threw her into the water.

Kendra surfaced, flailing her arms, and gave him a panicked look. "I can't swim! Help me!" She went under.

"Oh, shit!" Garth said, and dove in after her.

When he surfaced, he looked around, treading water, but couldn't find her. "Kendra!" he screamed, terrified she had gone under and wouldn't resurface.

He felt something underneath him, then grunted, "Unh!" as his legs were pushed forward and he toppled onto his back and under the water.

Garth came up, facing her.

Kendra, treading water quite nicely, laughed at him.

Garth's look turned stormy as he reached for her. "You're gonna pay for that!"

She shrieked and took off, but he quickly overpowered her and ducked her under.

She came up sputtering, and they splashed water at each other, laughing and shouting.

Before Garth knew it, she was in his arms and they were kissing passionately. Kendra made small, moaning sounds in the back of her throat as her mouth traveled his hungrily. Garth clutched her body to his, reveling in the feel of her lips on his, vaguely praying, Please, God, don't let this ever end.

Kendra suddenly opened her eyes, gave him a look he couldn't read, and pulled away.

"Keni?"

"I can't," she said, her words panicked. "I can't do this, Garth." She began crying, swam to shore, left the water, and ran to the cabin.

Garth stayed behind, cursing himself, letting the cold water cool his passion.

CHAPTER 25

▼

Tony was having a temper-tantrum; throwing papers around in his office, kicking at the desk, ranting and raving.

Vincent leaned against the door impassively, ignoring the alarmed looks Mark kept shooting his way, and watched Tony have his hissy fit.

Tony finally stopped, breathing heavily, turned, and caught the two of them staring at him. "What the hell are you two idiots doing in here? Get out there and find my wife!"

Mark, beating a hasty retreat, almost knocked into Vincent as he exited the door.

Vincent watched him leave, then closed the door and faced Tony.

Tony pointed his finger at him. "This is your fault. You left her alone in that car, you stupid shit."

Vincent held his hands up and shrugged his shoulders. "How was I to know she was gonna run, boss? Oh, wait, maybe it's 'cause you beat the crap out of her one too many times. You think that could be the reason?" His voice had turned acerbic.

Tony glared at him. "You got a problem with the way I treat my wife?"

"I got a problem with anybody beating up on an innocent. And the way I see it, the only thing your wife has ever done, Tony, is try to stand up for herself, what she believes in." Vincent knew he was treading dangerous ground but was unable to stop himself.

Tony stalked over to his desk, pulled out his leather chair, and sat down heavily in it. He was silent for a moment as he regarded Vincent, who stood calmly smoking his cigarette.

Vincent took one last, long drag on the cigarette, then put it out in a crystal ashtray on Tony's desk, blowing smoke into the air.

Tony continued to watch him.

Vincent leaned toward Tony. "How many times I had to stop you just shy of putting her in the hospital? How many times she ended up in the hospital 'cause I wasn't here?"

Tony's brow furrowed. "So, what, you made yourself her protector here?" He raised his eyebrows and leaned back in his chair.

"What'd she ever do to you, Tony, to warrant getting the crap beat out of her time after time?"

Tony shrugged. "She's my wife. It's her duty to obey me, to please me. And if she doesn't see fit to do what I want her to, if she disobeys me, she knows the price she pays for that. Nothing goes unpunished in my camp. You know that, Vin."

Vincent straightened up, looking angry. "Yeah, well, maybe you could have cut her some slack."

Tony rubbed his chin as he studied Vincent once more, then frowned with suspicion. "You got feelings for her?"

"I respect her, Tony," Vincent said, his voice hard. "Something you maybe don't understand, but I respect the hell out of someone who's got more backbone than any of these goons you got working for you." He swept his hand toward the closed door.

Tony smiled at this, pleased. "Yeah. I gotta say I respect the hell out of my Angel."

Vincent drew close again. "You want to blame somebody for her running from you the way she did, blame yourself, Tony. You know you're the reason she left. And if anything happens to her out there, she ends up dead or near-dead, it's your doing. You sent her out there so hurt she could hardly walk, but so desperate to get away from you, she went anyway, no coat, no money, no nothing but that damn, frigging car you seem so concerned about."

Visibly bristling at this, Tony gathered himself with a stormy look on his face. He was interrupted from replying by the ringing phone on his desk. He snatched it up after taking time to glare at Vincent. "Yeah?" He listened for a minute and his face rapidly changed from a scowl to a wide grin. He glanced back at Vincent and nodded.

Damn! Vincent thought to himself. He sat down in the chair across from Tony, shook out another cigarette and lit up, all the while watching and listening to his boss on the phone.

"Bring him and the car here," Tony said in a curt voice. "Now!" He hung up the phone.

"Where was it?"

"Some kid had it, joy-riding." Tony stood, strode over to his minibar, and fixed himself a drink.

"What'd he do, get pulled over for speeding?"

"Nah, got spotted going down Neyland Drive, right in front of the Thompson Boling Arena by a cop from KPD."

"One of your cops."

"Yeah, right. He's bringing him here now." Tony turned back to Vincent and held up his glass. "You want a drink?"

Vincent shook his head.

The policeman arrived fifteen minutes later and had in tow a tall, lanky, red-headed teenager who looked to be about seventeen, Vincent thought. He studied the kid, taking in the narrow shoulders, long neck, protruding Adam's apple, and nervous demeanor, thinking, What we got here is a young Ichibod Crane.

"That the one?" Tony asked the cop while staring at the teenager.

"Yep." The policeman glanced around Tony's office, appreciating the opportunity to be able to brag to his colleagues about having been allowed into the inner sanctum.

"Okay, you can go. I'll take care of you later." Tony waited for the cop to give him a respectful nod, then turn and leave. He softly closed the door behind him.

Tony approached the youngster, who was his height but about one hundred pounds lighter. "You know that was my car they found you in?" His voice was mild as he circled around the teenager.

"Um, not till the policeman told me, sir," young Ichibod said, his voice cracking.

Tony faced the boy and stared into his frightened eyes. "You know who I am?"

"Actually, sir, I'm just a high school student. I'm afraid I don't recognize the name."

Vincent smiled at this.

Tony glanced at Vincent, frowned at his humor, then turned his attention back to the young man. "What's your name?"

"Uh, James Gallaher, sir, but my friends call me Jimmy G." Jimmy began nervously tugging at his shirt.

"Well, James, let me make something clear to you. You stole the wrong car when you stole my car, you understanding me? I—"

"Uh, sir, I didn't actually, uh, steal the car, sir," Jimmy said in a shaky voice.

Tony looked at Vincent. "He says he didn't steal the car," he said, sounding in awe.

Vincent nodded. "Yeah, that's what I thought he said."

Jimmy seemed to notice Vincent then. His eyes widened slightly as he stared at him. He turned back to Tony. "I found it, sir. It had been—well, sir, I thought someone had abandoned it, so I just took it. Well, after I got it unstuck, I took it. Well, actually, I had to jump it off, you see, 'cause the battery was dead. And I was going to return it to the police department, but I got turned around somehow, you know, was going the wrong way—"

"Can the crap!"

Jimmy visibly startled.

Tony grabbed Jimmy by the collar, causing Vincent to tense. "You're going to tell me where you found that friggin' car and you're going to tell me when you found it and what you did after you found it, you hear me? And don't play games with me. I know you weren't gonna return the car!" Tony's voice seemed to be rising with each word spoken.

Jimmy's face was bright red and his eyes were filled with tears. He kept swallowing nervously, his hands twitched spastically, and he looked like all of a sudden he needed to use the bathroom. "Yes, sir. Yes, sir, I'll tell you everything, sir. Just, please, don't hurt me, sir, I didn't—"

"Shut up your whining and tell me where it was," Tony interrupted.

"In North Knoxville, on a ridge up behind that big truck stop and restaurant they have out there, right off Raccoon Valley." The words spilled from Jimmy in a frantic rush.

Tony turned to Vincent. "You know where he's talking about?"

Vincent nodded. "Yeah, that's a real popular place for truck drivers."

"Okay, it was on a ridge behind the truck stop, you're saying?" Tony asked Jimmy.

"Yes, sir, just sitting there. Well, someone had apparently thrown brush over it, looked like someone had tried to conceal it, you know. And looked like it had been buried in snow back when we had that blizzard, you know. It was still stuck in it good. But yeah, that's where I found it."

"When?"

Jimmy looked down at his feet and his hands did their spastic dance once more.

"When?" Tony roared, causing the boy to jump.

"A few months ago."

Tony took a moment, then gave him an incredulous look. "You've been driving it around for a few months?"

Jimmy glanced at Vincent, then looked at Tony. "No, sir. No, sir. I been trying to get it out of there for that long. It was stuck good. Where the snow had been, it had all turned to mud and ice, and that car was in deep, man. I been working forever trying to get it out. 'Course I didn't tell any of my friends about it, didn't want them to know about it, 'cause they would have stole it, you know. So I just did it on my own. Finally it dried up enough so I could get it out of there. Today's the first time I drove it, sir. I swear to you on the Bible."

Tony glowered. "You find anything in it?"

Jimmy gave him a confused look.

Tony cocked his head, gave him a deadly look.

"Only thing I found was the keys, sir, I swear."

Tony glanced at Vincent. "Anything you want to ask this retard?"

Vincent stood, walked up to Jimmy, and studied him openly. "Nah, boss. I think he's being truthful. Aren't you, James?"

Jimmy nodded.

Vincent turned to Tony. "If you don't have any other business with this young man, why don't I take James here outside, have Mark drive him home?"

Tony shook his head. "A kid goes stealing a car, riding around in it, we can't just let him off the hook that easy. He's got to be punished."

Vincent felt a twinge of alarm, seeing the look in Tony's eyes. "Punished? Hell, Tony, what do you think this kid's dad's gonna do to him, he finds out whose car he stole and went joy-riding in? He probably won't be sitting for awhile. Right, kid?" Vincent stared at Jimmy, daring him to state otherwise.

"Oh, God, I didn't think about my dad."

Tears were gathering in the teenager's eyes once more, and Vincent wondered if Jimmy was acting or really this scared of his old man. Then knew good ole Jimmy G. wasn't acting when he burst into tears. Damn, Vincent thought.

Tony watched Jimmy blubber for a moment. "Cop get your driver's license info?"

"Yes, sir, he sure did, sure, soon as he pulled me over." Jimmy wiped his nose and blinked his eyes.

Tony nodded distractedly, then headed toward the phone.

Vincent opened the door, waited for Jimmy to hurry through, then closed it, trying to get the kid out of there before Tony got the crazy notion to do him some kind of harm.

Mark was on his cell phone downstairs. Vincent caught his eye, cocked his head toward the door, and Mark followed him and Jimmy outside.

"Take this kid home," Vincent said. "Do it now unless you want to witness the same thing you saw in Florida."

Mark trotted off to retrieve the car.

Jimmy was shaking again. "Thank you, sir. That guy, he had me scared, you know. That look he had in his eyes, I was afraid he'd—"

"Shut up. Let me give you some advice, kid. Next time you get the urge to go joy-riding or take something that isn't yours, you think about what happened in there. You were this close to being taken out of here in the trunk of that car you stole, you understand?"

Jimmy's eyes widened. "Oh, man. I knew I'd pay for taking that car. I knew it when I got in it."

"Go," Vincent said as Mark pulled the car to the curb. He watched Jimmy climb in the front seat, caught the door before it shut, and leaned in. "One more thing, kid. Be sure and tell your old man what you did, and anything he dishes out, you take it and be glad that's all you're getting."

"Yes, sir," Jimmy G. said, tearing up again.

Vincent stepped back, closed the door, stood and saw the car out of sight before going back in to Tony.

CHAPTER 26

▼

Kendra's bedroom door was closed when Garth entered the house. He stood in the hall, water dripping from his hair and jeans, staring at this barrier, then shook his head slightly.

After changing into dry clothes, Garth went to the sunroom to stoke the fireplace with wood against the forthcoming chilly evening. He caught movement in the doorway, glanced up at Kendra, then returned to his chore.

Kendra came near and stood waiting patiently.

Garth finally finished and looked at her.

Kendra's face wore a pained expression. "I'm frigid," she said.

Garth didn't understand at first. "What?"

"I can't—I don't enjoy sex. I don't like it, to tell you the truth. That's why I—when we—I just wanted you to know that what happened, it wasn't your fault. It's me, Garth. Please don't take it personally."

Garth leaned against the mantel. "What are you talking about, Kendra?"

She walked away from him and sat in her favorite chair next to the windows. "It's what he did to me. You remember you asked me once how I came to be with Tony and I told you my dad owed him a favor and I was it? It's only fair I tell you the whole story, Garth. I owe it to you more than anyone, I guess."

Garth was silent as he continued to regard her, waiting to hear what she had to say.

"I've known Tony since I was ten. He and my father were in cahoots, I guess you could say. My dad was a farmer, owned a lot of acreage, and there was a hidden airstrip on his property Tony used for moving his firearms and drugs. He also grew marijuana there, with my dad." Kendra noticed Sarge sitting on the floor in front of the chair, staring at her. She reached down, scooped him up, put his face to hers, and kissed his forehead. She settled him in her lap and stroked his side, immediately eliciting loud noises of content from the cat.

Garth waited patiently.

"When I was younger, I really liked him. He'd bring me gifts when he came to see my father, always tell me what a beautiful girl I was, tease me, spend time with me. Something I never got from my own dad." She gave him an embarrassed look. "I just ate it up. I couldn't wait to see him, couldn't wait to see what he had brought me."

"You were just a kid, Keni."

Ignoring this, she continued. "I went to live with him when I was fourteen. My mother had disappeared, just run off, my dad said. He told me that he owed Tony for a favor he had done him, and the only payment he would accept was me." She glanced at Garth and the pain was evident on her face. "Tony wanted a wife, but that wife had to be the perfect mate for him. He wanted someone he could train how to act, how to look, so what better way than to take a young girl who meets whatever parameters you have set for that wife and mold her into who you want her to be?" Her tone was sarcastic.

"That's archaic," Garth breathed.

"Tony told me from the start that he was grooming me to be his wife. I felt honored that someone who seemed so important, so powerful, so rich would want me. He insisted I be well-educated, but he wouldn't let me attend school, he wouldn't let me out of his sight, actually, so he hired all these teachers and tutors to come in and teach me. I had everything I ever dreamed of. I took ballet lessons, horseback riding lessons, swimming lessons, piano, the flute. I had my own room, my own TV, stereo system, computer, movies, all kinds of clothes, anything I wanted. And I loved it at first, to tell you the truth." She sat silently, lost in thought.

Garth shifted position, causing her to glance at him. "I learned very quickly that when you live with Tony, you live by his rules. He is dictator supreme. No one defies him, no one disobeys him, because if you do, you are severely punished. And he likes to punish."

Garth noticed her face was flushed.

"It was humiliating, what he did to me," she said in an angry voice. "But I'd tell myself that it could be worse, I could be home with my dad, enduring his belt." She looked up and wiped tears from her eyes.

"Ah, Keni."

"I learned to live with it, telling myself the good outweighed the bad, trying to behave, trying to become who he wanted me to become. Until one day when I was eighteen, my dad showed up. I heard arguing in Tony's study and was curious as to what was going on. I overheard my father telling Tony that the DEA was all over his farm and he needed to know where my mother's body was buried so he could dig her up before they found her." She looked at him. "He killed my mother, Garth. That's the favor my father owed him for."

"My God."

"When I heard that, I just went crazy. I grabbed a knife from the kitchen, went into the study, and stabbed Tony with it. But not hard enough, just barely grazed him, actually. And that was the first time he beat me. I woke up in the hospital, and when I came home, Tony told me I had married him while I was in the hospital, which I didn't remember at all. He said my dad had taken off and he was the only family I had now. Then he told me that as his wife, I couldn't testify against him, and after that, he made damn sure I didn't move without someone knowing about it."

Garth knelt beside her and touched her arm. "Keni, I'm sorry," he said in a low voice.

She looked at him. "About my mother? She was the only person I thought truly loved me, up until she disappeared. But looking back on it now, I wonder how she could have stood by and let my dad treat me the way he did and not tried to interfere. Who can let someone do that to their own child?"

"I don't know," Garth said in a miserable voice.

Kendra wiped at her eyes.

"What happened after he took you home?"

She glanced at him, then away. "He told me since we were married, I now had to be a wife to him. I told him I hated him, that I wanted nothing more to do with him, so he raped me. I was only eighteen, Garth, and he raped me over and over again. And every time after that when he—he had sex with me, he raped me. Eventually, I learned not to fight him, that that's what he wanted me to do, so I'd just lie there and take it, endure it." Her voice rose at this. "And even that made him mad. Sometimes he beat me for that." She glanced at him. "He couldn't understand why I didn't respond to him, why I didn't want to have sex with him. God, I hated him so, couldn't stand for him to touch me." She looked at him miserably. "He always had his mistresses, his whores, even when I was younger, and it didn't stop after we were married." She emitted a harsh laugh. "I was so thankful for those women. But sooner or later, he would come to my bed, demanding I be a wife to him, making me do things to him, with him, things that were horrible." She stopped, breathing heavily. "He hurt me," she finally said, her voice hitching. "He made me hate the thought of it."

Garth took her hand.

She gazed intently at him. "I know how it's supposed to be between a man and a woman. I mean, I've read about it, about the feelings and the wonderment of it all, but I never felt that."

"Of course you didn't."

"I don't think I'll ever feel that, Garth. He made sure of that." Tears were rolling down her face. She withdrew her hand from his, gently picked up Sarge and placed him aside, then rose and went to her bedroom.

Kendra stayed in her room until the next morning, and all that day, she seemed shy and tense with him. Garth went about his business, letting her have her space and time. He wanted to talk to her about what she had told him; wanted to explain to her that what had happened to her was terrible, horrible, not her fault; wanted to tell her he would help her, do anything in the world for her, but kept quiet, hoping she knew this without him saying it.

She stayed close to him, though, assisting him with the chores in the barn, mucking out the stalls, feeding the horses, bringing in fresh water, helping him with downed fencing, piling up the firewood as he cut it. He noticed the way she would look at him from time to time, as if confused, as if puzzling something through. It was all he could do to keep his mouth shut. When he went to bed that night, he decided, the next morning, he would talk to her whether she wanted to or not.

CHAPTER 27

▼

The smell of days-old, greasy food intermingled with cigarette smoke and stale sweat assaulted their olfactory senses immediately upon entering the restaurant.

Tony glanced at Vincent. "Who could stand to eat in a dump like this?" he muttered.

Vincent chose not to respond.

They approached a man standing behind a long, chipped formica counter running two-thirds the length of the room. His belly bulged in front of him, straining obscenely against a food-stained apron that in better days had been white. His dark hair lay against his forehead in a lank, greasy wad. A cigarette was dangling out of one side of his mouth, and he was cleaning his fingernails with a pocketknife, trying to study the two men without appearing to.

Vincent stood across from the cook and waited patiently for him to meet his gaze. The man studiously picked dirt from beneath his right little finger, taking his time, then lazily raised his eyes, squinting at the trail of smoke spiraling upward.

Vincent glanced at the ash on the tip of the cigarette, mildly amazed that such a long length of dead tobacco could hold its shape as long as it had. He nodded at the cook. "Wonder if you could answer a few questions for me."

The man looked at Tony, then back to Vincent. "Don't know what I could tell you, whatever it is you're wanting to know." His eyes gleamed defiantly. He folded the blade of the knife into its niche and stuffed it in his back pocket. He finally removed the cigarette from his mouth and the ash daintily filtered down the front of his apron, looking to Vincent like spiraling gray flakes of dandruff.

Tony took his time pulling out his money clip, showing the man the wad of bills contained therein. He plucked out a hundred-dollar bill and held it toward the cook as he glared at him. "Won't hurt to try."

The man stuck the cigarette back in his mouth and grabbed the money, giving Tony an uneasy look.

Vincent wondered briefly whether he took the bill from greed or the look Tony was giving him.

Vincent held the picture of Angel in front of the cook's eyes. "You remember seeing this woman in here?" he asked, hoping not.

The cook glanced at the picture, once more pulled the cigarette out of his mouth after taking a drag, and threw it on the floor. He ground it out with his shoe as he expelled cigarette smoke. He took his time studying the picture, then said, "Maybe I have and maybe I haven't," giving them a smart-ass smirk.

Tony reached forward, grabbed his t-shirt, and pulled him close. "You want to think long and hard about how you answer him, 'cause we aren't here to play games, you understand? This is serious business and I'm not gonna stand around watching you act the wise-ass."

Tony nodded at Vincent, who pulled open his suit coat to reveal the holster lying beneath his left arm.

The cook's eyes widened considerably. "Okay, okay," he said, his voice barely a whisper.

Tony released him with a shove.

The man looked around, wide-eyed, as if for help. Everyone in the joint seemed to be busy doing something else. He glanced at Tony, then back at the picture. This time he seemed to study it intently. He gave Vincent an anxious look. "No, I don't remember seeing her. And believe me, a woman looks like that, I'd remember." He hesitated when Tony shifted restlessly.

Vincent lowered the picture. "This would have been around November. Any waitresses in here who were working then?"

The cook cast his eyes around the room before pointing to a matronly looking woman standing at the far end of the counter. She had her back to them, arms folded, and was staring out the window.

"Call her down here," Tony said in a gruff voice.

"Hey, Beulah!" the cook bellowed.

She turned slowly and gave their group a baleful look.

The cook cocked his head toward Tony. "Guy here needs to talk to you."

Beulah walked toward them, staring sullenly at the cook, then Tony and Vincent in turn. Her hair was a burnt orange color, teased in a style from the '60's,

Vincent was sure. She was short and squat, with a face that looked like it had seen better times. Her mouth seemed to be perpetually downcast, her chin having formed deep gouges to compensate for the shift in her skin. Her eyebrows were painted-on brown arches over small, beady, pale-blue eyes. She had a way about her that made Vincent tired just looking at her.

Beulah stopped in front of them and turned to Vincent, ignoring the cook and Tony. "What can I do for you?"

Vincent was shocked by her voice, which was low, husky, sexy. "Damn, girl, you ought to be on the radio," he said, going for nice.

She was pleased by this compliment. Her eyes lit up and her smile revealed yellowed teeth. Smoker's teeth, Vincent thought, followed by, That's where the huskiness comes from, I bet.

"Been there, done that," she answered. She glanced at Tony, then focused on Vincent.

Vincent nodded and held the picture out to her. "This woman would have been in here back in November sometime." He watched her eyes flash for a moment, then immediately become blank. "You seen her?" He knew she had and hoped Tony hadn't caught the guardedness.

Beulah shifted and placed a hand on one hip while studying the picture. "Nope, don't know as I recognize that one." She kept her attention on Vincent and ignored Tony. "We don't see that many classy ladies in here, if you get my gist." She indicated with her head the outlying restaurant area.

Vincent nodded, relieved.

Tony stepped toward her. "Maybe you ought to take a look at that picture again, lady, 'cause I think maybe you have seen this woman."

Beulah darted a glance at Tony, then at the picture. "Looks like a movie star to me." She shrugged. "Nope, I don't recognize her." She wouldn't look at Tony, who was bristling.

The cook moved away as quietly as he could.

Tony glared at the waitress in an effort to intimidate her. She wasn't buying it and gave him an irritated look in return.

"Look at it again," Tony insisted.

Beulah glowered at him. "Look, mister, one thing I make it a point to do is to stay out of other people's business. I see someone, I don't remember them two minutes after they've walked out that door. Deliberately, okay? I find life's a hell of a lot safer that way. If I saw her, I wouldn't remember her, deliberately. So, I can't help you. How many times I got to tell you that? Now, if you don't mind, I got customers I need to see to."

"Sure, sure. Sorry we bothered you." Vincent glanced at Tony, who was scowling at him.

After she left, Tony turned on his heel and stalked out the door. Vincent followed behind. They got in the car, Vincent behind the wheel, Tony in the passenger seat.

"What the hell did you think you were doing in there?" Tony exploded at him.

Vincent pushed in the lighter, reached into his jacket pocket, and pulled out his cigarette pack. "She said she didn't recognize her." He shook out a cigarette and placed it in his mouth.

"She was lying."

"What are you gonna do, Tony, beat the truth out of her in front of all those people in there?" Vincent asked truculently.

Tony gave him a disbelieving look. "It might behoove you to remember who the hell you're talking to." His voice was low, menacing.

The lighter popped out and Vincent took the time to light his cigarette, then replaced it. "Yeah, well, maybe you're letting your worries over Angel interfere with the logical thing to do here."

Tony glared.

"Listen, Tony, we're all worried about Angel. I know how much you love her, how much of a strain this has been on you, how much you want to find her. But you can't go around beating up on people 'cause they're not Angel or don't give you the information you want."

"Who the hell are you to tell me what to do?"

Vincent took the time to crack the window and blow smoke, then turned to Tony. "I'm the one trying to keep you from getting yourself into some real trouble here. What I have done ever since I've worked for you. I'm not trying to tell you what to do and you know it. I'm just trying to offer some logical advice."

Tony huffed.

"She said she didn't recognize Angel, so let it go, Tony. There's other waitresses in there, other people we can talk to. Truck drivers in and out of here all the time. Put some people out here, talking to them, showing her picture around. Sooner or later, you'll hit something. You know you will."

"I don't have the patience to wait and see if anybody shows up who maybe saw her. That bitch in there recognized the picture. I saw the way her eyes changed. She's the one we need to talk to."

"You want to talk to her, go ahead. But anything happens to her, you were seen talking to her, and you know they'll come looking for you."

Tony thought for a minute and finally shook his head. "Okay, here's what we'll do. I'll get Mark over here, put him on her till she leaves, have him follow her home, then we'll pay her a visit there."

Vincent looked with askance at him. "Did you hear what I just said to you? You were seen talking to her, and if something happens to her, they'll connect it to you right off the bat."

Tony was surprised Vincent was being so adamant about this. He usually just took orders or turned his head the other way when he didn't agree with what Tony was doing.

But Vincent wasn't through. "I been with you for years, Tony, and I been there for you, cleaned up your messes. But I'm telling you, I ain't gonna participate in anything else like that crap that went down in Florida. You raped and beat and then killed an innocent girl simply because she looked like Angel. And you got that look in your eyes now, tells me you'll kill this waitress if that's what it takes to get what you want from her. But I don't want any part of it. I'm your bodyguard and I'll do my job and I'll chauffeur you around, but don't ask or expect me to do any more than that. I won't be involved with killing another innocent person."

"You work for me and you'll do what I tell you!" Tony thundered.

"Within reason. You're gonna go down, Tony, you keep screwing up like this, and I don't intend to go down with you."

Tony thought a minute. "Okay, just take me home. I'll take care of this, send Mark and a couple of others guys over here, let them flash Angel's picture around." And take care of that waitress without your help, he finished to himself.

When they arrived at the estate, Tony told Vincent he wouldn't need him anymore that day, then called Mark into his study. He described Beulah to him, instructed him to stake out the restaurant, follow Beulah home, call him, and they'd go from there.

Mark, who now didn't hold Tony in such high esteem, went off praying Tony wasn't going to do any killing tonight.

CHAPTER 28

▼

They were in the aftermath of love, resting side by side, each smoking a cigarette, sharing a ceramic ashtray lying on the bed between their sweat-sheathed bodies.

Vincent ground out his cigarette, glanced at Chloe, and said, as if speaking to himself, "Something's gonna have to be done about Tony."

Chloe, who was his lawyer as well as lover, gave him a startled look. It was an unspoken rule between them that he didn't talk about what he did or who he worked for. She didn't want to know anything unless it had to do with legal defense involving Vinnie, which seemed to happen more often that not, considering he was associated with Tony. She rolled on her side and crushed out her cigarette, watching him, waiting to see if he was going to follow up.

Vincent glanced at her.

Chloe raised her eyebrows as if to say, "Well?"

"He's out of control," Vincent explained, and proceeded to tell her about the young woman in Florida.

Chloe sat up during his discourse, her face alternately reflecting anger and disgust. After he had finished, she frowned at him.

"I know," he said, answering her look. "I should have stopped him. You don't have to say it."

"And?"

Vincent only shook his head.

"My God, Vinnie, you stood outside that door and listened to that man rape, then murder that young girl and didn't do a thing to stop him!" she screamed at him.

Vincent, even though he felt he deserved the accusation, fought the urge to defend himself.

"What kind of man are you?"

He glared at her. "A killer, that's what, and don't tell me that's not one of the things you find attractive about me. Hell, we both know it's not my face."

Chloe lunged off the bed, stalked to the bathroom door, and flung it open. She grabbed her short, silk robe from the hook on the other side and put it on with jerky movements, glaring at him.

He was right. There was a dangerousness in Vinnie she found appealing, something Chloe hadn't wanted to admit to herself. She knew he had been involved in more than being Tony's bodyguard, but had never asked him to tell her, never wanted him to verify he was what she suspected him to be, what actually lured her to him, a cold-blooded murderer, like the man he worked for.

Vincent watched her, waiting for her tantrum to be over.

Chloe stalked up to him.

"Before you go any further," Vincent said, taking his cigarette pack off the nightstand without even looking at it, his eyes holding hers. "Before you say something you might regret later," he continued, shaking the pack, exposing a cigarette, pulling it out, his eyes cold, deadly, picking up the cigarette lighter from the nightstand, "remember who you're talking to here. All I want from you is honesty, Chloe, nothing else. That's all I've ever wanted. You understand me?"

That stopped her. She chewed on the inside of her cheek, a sign he knew meant she was mulling over what he had said to her.

Chloe finally gave him a sullen look. "You gonna kill me now that I know this crap?"

"You're my lawyer. This would fall under attorney/client privilege, I do believe." Vincent lit the cigarette, then returned the lighter back to the nightstand. His eyes squinted at the smoke trailing upwards but never left hers.

Chloe turned around to break eye contact, aware she was now very attracted to him, knowing he had told her something deadly incriminating here, something that could get her killed, if he so desired. God, I am so sick, she thought to herself with disgust as she plopped down in the rocking chair across the room from him and brought her eyes back to his.

They stared at one another.

Vincent finally nodded, reading the look she was giving him.

She cocked her head at him. "Do you love me, Vinnie? Do you have any feelings for me other than someone to lay when the mood hits?"

Vincent regarded her, aware she knew hardly anything about him, of the feelings he had for her. She was a knockout, he thought, possessing an exotic beauty she did not appreciate. Her eyes were dark, almost black, matched by her long, coarse hair. Her facial features were sharp, angular, exquisite; her body was long, willowy. She was almost as tall as Vinnie and he found that incredibly sexy. He often wondered to himself why she seemed so fond of him, a stocky, broadly-built, bald-headed criminal. And as he had just expressed to her, that's what he had come to believe, that she was attracted to him for what he did, not who he was.

Chloe waited, watching him smoke his cigarette, watching his eyes travel over her body.

He finally shrugged. "I guess I have more feelings for you than I want, to be honest about it."

He was surprised when she threw her head back and laughed at this.

Chloe rose and walked toward him, untying her robe. It fell open to reveal the swell of one breast, the muscles in one long thigh.

Vincent itched to reach his hands out, place them there.

Chloe climbed on the bed and straddled him, then pulled her robe further apart to reveal her nakedness. "Well, here's some news for you, kiddo." She placed her hands on his chest, leaned down, and kissed him gently. She smiled when his hands cupped her breasts, feeling so good, so warm, so natural. If only bras could feel this good, she fleetingly thought to herself.

She raised up and gazed into his eyes. "I admit, I'm attracted to that dark, ominous side of yours, Vincent. But there's also a gentle side I'm attracted to even more, the side you show me when we make love and you're in the right kind of mood." She stretched herself out flat on top of him and brought her face close to his. "I love the way you look."

Vincent was surprised at this. They hardly ever exchanged any kind of niceties between them, treating each other professionally until they were actually in bed, engaged in physical pleasure with one another.

Her eyes held his. "I love the way you present yourself, the way you've educated yourself, are always reaching out culturally, trying to better yourself."

He put his hands in her hair.

She smiled slightly. "But even more, I love your passion, Vinnie, the way you make my body feel, the things you do to my body, the way you use my body, the way you seem to always know what I want from you." She kissed him now in a way that told him she wanted him to be rough and crude and demanding, a role he could play very well.

Afterwards, Chloe lay on her stomach and watched Vincent light another cig-arette, her body tingling and pulsing and throbbing. She appreciated the fact that he responded to her needs the way she wanted him to but was aware that they were maybe not such healthy needs to have.

She finally raised up, pulled the cigarette away from him, took a drag, then placed it back in his mouth. "Why didn't you do anything?"

"Wasn't the time."

"What would you have done if that had been Angel?" Chloe was aware of Vin-nie's respect for Tony's wife.

"Killed him," he answered, his voice rough.

"So why didn't you kill him then?"

"Too much explaining to do. Mark was there, others knew where we were, what we were doing there. Just wasn't the right time."

"How'd you feel, out there, listening to that?"

He turned his head, looked at her.

"I'm not criticizing you. I'm just curious. How'd that make you feel?"

"Like he needs to die." Vincent turned away from her, crushed the cigarette, then lay on his back, studying the ceiling.

"So, if that had been Angel in there, you would have killed him anyway?" she asked, not letting it go.

"If that's the only way I could have stopped him, yeah."

"Why, Vinnie? What's so special about Angel that you'd risk your life for her?" Although Vincent had never told her he deliberately had let Angel escape from Tony, Chloe had suspected as much. His battered face and body had been evidence enough for that confirmation.

He lay there, thinking, then began speaking in a soft voice. "Did I ever tell you about my little sister, Maria?" Not waiting for a response, he continued. "She was the light of my life, man, when I was a kid. Maria was two years younger than me, this tiny, precocious kid running around, following me everywhere, looking up at me with these huge, dark eyes. Told everybody I was her hero. We'd be walking down the street, she'd be stopping people going by, saying, 'This is Vinnie, my big brother, he's my hero.'" He stopped, smiling slightly. "Man, I loved that kid," he said in a low voice.

"What happened to her?" Chloe asked softly, afraid he'd stop talking. Vincent was a guarded man and this was the first time he had ever mentioned a sister to her.

"We grew up poor," he said, as if he hadn't heard her. "Lived in the projects, where I belonged to this gang. I mean, you live in the projects, that's what you do. But Maria had decided by that time she was going to be a nun, going to devote her life to God, do only good things for people." He shook his head. "I tried my damnedest to talk her out of that, but she was determined. She said God talked to her, said he wanted her to become a nun, and that's what she was going to do."

For the fist time since she had known him, Chloe thought she saw a hint of tears in Vincent's eyes.

"She always had this, I don't know, sereneness about her, this calmness. It was beautiful in a way. She hated it that I joined that gang. She told me it was the devil's work at play, and she was probably right. I promised her as soon as I turned eighteen, I was going to move out, take her with me, send her to school while I worked, put her through college, all that. Man, we made such plans together; stupid, immature plans." Vincent stopped, reminiscing.

Chloe put her hand on his face and turned him toward her.

"She always went to mass, never missed it unless she was sick, and I always met her there and walked her home. I was late one time, and so, I guess she started walking home on her own. I got to the church, couldn't find her, and went looking for her. Found her a couple of blocks away in an alley, raped, beaten, bleeding everywhere." His voice had become strained, and he paused, his mouth working.

Chloe had tears in her eyes. "Oh, Vinnie, I'm so sorry."

"I picked her up, took her to the hospital—ran to the hospital, about half a mile away. She was unconscious till we got there, but when I put her down on the gurney, she opened her eyes and looked at me. You know what she said to the nurse? 'This is Vinnie, my brother, he's my hero.'" His voice broke and he wiped angrily at his eyes. "Then she said, 'I knew you'd come Vinnie, I knew you'd find me.' I asked her who had done this to her, and right before she died, she gave me the three names after she made me promise I'd forgive them."

Vincent paused once more, tears running down his face.

Chloe wiped his face gently with her hands. "And did you? Forgive them?"

"Yeah, I forgave them, all right. Tracked them all three down, took them one by one to the alley they took her to, raped them with a knife the way they did her, then beat them to death and left them for the rats."

Chloe nodded, thinking, Good for you. She waited until Vincent had better control of himself. "Angel's like Maria, she has that same sereneness, calmness you talked about."

"Yeah, exactly. But it's more than that. Maria was a fighter. She wouldn't back down to anyone. She had backbone, just like Angel. Maria'd stand up to my old man when he was in a drunken snit, knowing he'd beat the crap out of her, but she'd do it anyway. And if he was beating on me, she'd try to stop him, knowing she was going to get hurt." He shook his head. "I've seen Angel stand up to Tony countless times knowing she was going to get the crap knocked out of her or end up in the hospital if she didn't back down, but she never did. Always stood her ground, just like my Maria did. And has this huge belief in God, even though, the way I see it, their God hasn't been so nice to either her or Maria. But they both share this deep love, I guess, for their God. Something I can't understand for the life of me."

"But respect the hell out of," Chloe finished.

He looked at her. "Yeah. Like that. Plus Angel's always treated me with respect, like I'm part of her family, which I don't get, since it's Tony I work for."

"Maybe Angel sees in you what Maria did."

Vincent didn't reply.

Chloe studied him a moment, then shifted against him, raising up on one elbow. "You let her go, didn't you?"

He brought his eyes to her but remained mute.

Vincent hadn't been present in the home when Angel had told Tony about the baby. He thought, if he had been, things wouldn't have progressed to the point they did. But he had been away, off on a business trip up North for his boss. And when he came back, Angel was in the hospital, Tony telling him on the way to bring her home that she had had a miscarriage. Not acting concerned about it.

Vincent didn't pick up on what actually happened until he was in her room, helping the nurse load the numerous flower arrangements on a cart to be delivered to other patients, at Angel's direction. He happened to look up and saw Tony, who was now playing the solicitous husband, try to take hold of his wife's arm. He watched her jerk her arm out of his grasp as she glared at him, watched her lips move to say the word, "Murderer." His eyes then shifted to Tony for his reaction, which was a defensive gesture of dismissal. Then back to Angel's, seeing her turn her red-rimmed, swollen eyes to his, her hands going to her abdomen, the pain and anguish on her face so obviously readable. They stared at one another for just a second or so, but Vincent knew in that short amount of time that there had been no miscarriage, more like an abortion brought on by her husband. His eyes shifted to Tony, who was now busy with Angel's luggage, then back to Angel, his eyebrows raised. She had given him a barely perceptible nod, then turned away from him.

An anger swelled in him which he hadn't felt since his kid sister had been murdered. In Vincent's eyes, you didn't kill innocents, as his Maria had been.

And there was no more innocent being on earth than a child; an unborn one at that.

Vincent had helped Angel into her sweater, then had escorted her and Tony downstairs, and did not fail to notice the way Angel shifted away from Tony when he would try to get near her.

Tony had instructed Vincent to get the car while he and Angel waited under the alcove. Vincent turned and looked at Angel one more time, wishing he could send her the message this would not go unpunished. But she wasn't looking at him; her eyes were downcast, turned to her now-empty abdomen.

Vincent brought the car around, noticed Tony was busily engaged in conversation with Angel's doctor. He escorted Angel to the back passenger door, helped her inside, and closed the door. He opened the driver's side door and settled in behind the wheel. Their eyes met in the rear-view mirror. He glanced to see where Tony was before saying, "Angel, I'm gonna step outside, smoke a cigarette while the car warms up. You think you'll be okay?"

Her eyes widened slightly, knowing in an instant what he was offering her. "He won't let this go unpunished," she whispered.

Vincent shook his head in a dismissive gesture. His hand traveled to the door handle, then hesitated. He looked into the rear-view mirror once more. "When I get out, engage all the locks." He pulled out his wallet. "All I got's a couple of hundreds," he said, placing them on the seat, returning his wallet to his jacket pocket. "Drive away fast. When you get to wherever you go, I'll send more money to you. Just call my cell phone number, all right?"

She nodded, tears coming to her eyes.

"He'll pay for this," Vincent said in a hard voice. "I'll make sure of it."

She was openly crying now. "Thank you, Vinnie."

"Move, quick." He lunged out and stepped away, his back to the car, pulling out his pack of cigarettes. When the front door closed and the locks engaged, he smiled to himself as he tugged one out and stuck it in his mouth. Hearing the car shift into gear, then accelerate, he finally turned around and tried to act surprised.

Vincent smiled to himself now, in bed with Chloe, remembering how great that had felt.

"You knew Tony would make you pay. I mean, I saw you afterward. You were in pretty bad shape. What made you help her at that point?" Chloe asked, bringing him back to the here and now.

Vincent reached for the cigarettes again, and said, his voice pressured, "He killed her baby."

Chloe stared at him, trying to understand this man, this murderer, who seemed to be two different people to her. "She was pregnant?"

Vincent lit the cigarette, took a drag and cocked his mouth sideways to blow smoke away from Chloe. "Yeah. I guess one of the times Tony took her, he didn't use the proper precaution." He glanced at Chloe, then away. "I suspected, you know. A lot of mornings at breakfast, I noticed she didn't eat much, had this queasy look on her face. But she had this glow about her, Chloe. I mean, man, I've read about that glow pregnant women get but I never saw it till Angel. She caught me looking at her one morning. I raised my eyebrows, you know, kind of asking. She shook her head at me, then glanced at Tony, and I knew then she was afraid for him to find out."

"What'd he do when he did?"

"Beat the crap out of her, gave her a miscarriage, that's what that son of a bitch did. If I had been there, I'd have killed him then. There's nothing in life lower than a man who kills an innocent."

Chloe stared at him, surprised at this. "And I take it the people you yourself have killed aren't innocents?"

He frowned at her. "Hell, no, Chloe. I kill men only and corrupt men at that. Men who present a danger to Tony or his family. That's my freaking job, in case you hadn't figured that out yet."

She studied him, then lay on her back. "This is what I've gotten myself into," she said more to herself than him, "in love with a killer who's choosy."

Vincent reached out and traced her face with the back of one hand. "Who I kill isn't the only thing I'm choosy about, baby."

Chloe smiled.

Much later, she asked, "So, this problem with Tony, who's going to be the one to handle that?" She was starting to worry now.

"I'll take care of Tony," Vincent said, ending the discussion.

CHAPTER 29

▼

Mark called Tony that evening at eight. "I trailed her home. Looks like she's in for the night."

"You're sure?"

"Looks it. I peeked in her window a minute ago. She's sitting in front of the TV in a robe, drinking a beer."

Tony thought about calling Vinnie, having him drive him over to Beulah's house, but after their discussion this afternoon, he wasn't so sure Vinnie would cooperate with what he had in mind. Besides, he told himself, Vinnie was visiting his girlfriend. Let him have some screw time. Maybe he'd be in a better mood next time he saw him. He could handle this on his own with Mark. So he told Mark to come pick him up.

Tony instructed Mark to park on the street running parallel to the back of Beulah's house. They sat in the car strategizing, finally decided to wait until it was good and dark and most everyone was in for the night before they approached the waitress.

Mark was nervous, edgy. He didn't want Tony to know how agitated he was and had to literally force himself to sit still and not squirm around. He was now more afraid of Tony than ever, after what had happened in Florida. He had taken to heart what Vincent had told him, that Tony would do to him what he had done to the Angel surrogate. Mark now saw Tony as a crazy killer, not the strong, powerful figure he had once imagined him to be.

At ten, they exited the car and, under cover of darkness, making sure to stay in the shadows, crept to Beulah's house. They stood in the umbra of a huge maple at the edge of her property and studied the domicile, a one-story, red-brick, cracker-box replica of the houses surrounding it. There weren't any lights on in the back.

"Where was she watching TV at?" Tony whispered.

"The living room, in the front."

There was a door in the back of the house leading to a small, covered porch. They decided that must be the kitchen.

"We'll try that door first," Tony said.

Staying in shadows, they managed to make their way to the back of the house. Tony indicated with his head for Mark to try the door. It was locked, of course.

Tony was now wishing he had brought Vinnie, who could pick a lock in a second. Mark reached out and shook the door slightly. Both were astonished to see it move.

"Keep doing that," Tony whispered. "Maybe the lock's not engaged all the way or it's flimsy."

Mark shook the door back and forth, then finally lifted up on it. It surprised him when it snicked open.

They stood at the gaping door, listening. There were mumblings from the TV in the front room, but nothing else.

Tony glanced around the neighborhood, making sure no one was watching them, then cocked his head, indicating for Mark to enter.

After they were both inside the kitchen, Tony made sure to quietly close and relock the door behind them, then walked toward the faintly pulsating bluish light coming from the front of the house. Mark reluctantly followed behind.

Tony boldly stepped into the living room and was startled to see a small, yipping animal coming at him. He kicked it away, hearing high-pitched yelping in response.

Beulah, who had been half-asleep on the couch, sat up, looking frightened at the sight of a man coming into her house. She grew angry when she recognized who it was, then worried at the sounds her small dog was making. She immediately stood, picked up the animal, and murmured comfortingly to it.

Tony grinned at knowing what her weak spot was.

Beulah held the dog, which was now issuing small whimpers, close to her face and glared at Tony. "You didn't have to hurt him."

Tony gave her a wicked grin. "You ought to teach that mutt some manners."

Beulah drew back from that smile.

"You know why we're here," Tony said.

Beulah only then realized there was another man, catching sight of Mark standing behind and slightly to the side of Tony. She felt defeated when she realized it wasn't the one who had been in the restaurant earlier that day, the man who acted like he had some sense.

Beulah sent Tony a stubborn look. "I told you, I don't remember that girl."

Tony looked surprised. "You gonna hold onto that story?"

Beulah remained silent as her eyes shifted from Tony to Mark, then back again.

Tony turned to Mark. "Get the dog."

Mark approached Beulah, who was clutching the animal to her chest, trying to protect him.

"What do you want my dog for?" she yelled at Tony. "He ain't done nothing." Her eyes shifted to Mark. "Please, mister, don't take my dog. Please, don't take him." She cried out as Mark put his hands around the little mutt and tugged. The dog began to whine with pain as the two struggled over him. Seeing she was hurting the only thing in the world she loved at this point, Beulah let go, not wanting to harm her baby.

Mark grabbed the dog away and returned to Tony's side.

"Where'd she go?" Tony asked Beulah, who was now openly crying.

"I don't know, mister. Like I told you, I try to stay out of everybody else's business."

Tony reached out, grabbed one of the dog's legs, and twisted it in his hand, snapping it like a twig.

Mark winced at the sound.

The dog cried out, then began squirming in agony, causing Beulah to bawl even louder.

Tony waited for her wailing to cease. "Each time I ask you that question and you tell me you don't know, I'm gonna break another leg. After that, I'll break the damn creature's neck."

Beulah held out her arms beseechingly. "Please, don't hurt my baby."

Tony glanced at Mark. "Put your hand around his muzzle. I don't want him to bite me." He looked back at Beulah. "When'd you see her and where did she go?" He placed his hand around another leg.

Beulah wrung her hands with despair. She had liked Kendra when she came into the restaurant, liked her gentle manner, her quiet repose, the classy way she looked and acted, the way she treated Beulah with great respect. Beulah didn't get that from many people these days. She had suspected right off the bat that the woman was running from something or someone and had made a vow to herself not to let that person know where she had gone. But her love for the dog out-weighed her concern for the woman she had only met once and talked to for thirty minutes or so. "Okay, okay, I'll tell you," she said, tears running down her face.

Tony waited.

"Please, let me have him."

Tony gave her a shark's grin. "You tell me what I want to know first, then you can have him."

Beulah kept wringing her hands and cringing at the sounds of pain the dog was making. "I don't know her name, but she came into the truck stop back in November, like you said. I don't remember the day. She was looking for a truck driver to give her a ride. I felt sorry for her 'cause it was so cold outside, getting ready to snow, and she didn't have a coat or nothing. She was freezing when she came in, and I gave her some hot chocolate to try to warm her up." She looked with longing at the dog, who had stopped thrashing in Mark's arms and was now making muffled, whimpering noises.

"And?" Tony prompted.

Beulah startled, then turned her attention back to him. "There was this truck driver, he only comes through once a year, he was in there, heading to North Carolina. He picks up Christmas trees, delivers them, then goes back home. I seen them two talking, and she left with him. I swear, mister, I don't know nothing more than that."

Tony was scowling. "What was the name of the driver?"

Beulah looked agitated. "I only know his first name. It's Luke. Like I said, we only see him once a year. He always comes by, though, on his way to North Carolina. A real nice guy. He'll do just about anything for anybody. I've seen him help other people, too, you know, in trouble…" Her voice trailed off.

"Where's he from?"

Beulah thought. "I know his regular run's from Texas to California. I guess he lives in one of them states, wouldn't you say?" She looked pleadingly at Tony.

"Okay, we got us a Luke from either Texas or California who's a truck driver." Tony glanced at the dog, then back to Beulah. "That doesn't tell me anything." His voice was low, almost soothing.

Tony could practically see Beulah's brain working frantically, trying to recall more information. Damn, what people will do for their animals, he thought with disgust.

Beulah's face brightened, and he knew she had remembered something.

"I recollect the name on the side of his truck," she said, almost triumphantly. "He works for Southwest Regional Logistics, I think is the name of it. Something like that. Oh, and I think I heard somebody call him Driver, one time. That's the name he uses on the CB. Surely, mister, you can find him that way. He ought to be able to tell you where your young lady went."

Tony studied Beulah while contemplating. He could tell she had exhausted her memory for anything concerning his Angel and where she went. He debated on killing the dog or not. On killing her or not. But as Vinnie had pointed out earlier, he had been seen talking to her. If she hadn't told him the truth and he had already killed the dog, he wouldn't have a bargaining point. Glancing around the room, he thought, Living the life she does, I doubt if threatening her with her own life would do any good.

Tony turned to Mark, grabbed the dog by the scruff of the neck, and held it up in the air. The dog squirmed and tried to get out of his hold, making shrill whimpering noises.

Beulah began to cry openly and held out her arms for her precious animal.

Tony waited for her to meet his eyes. When she did, he said, "I ought to punish you for not being honest with me earlier."

Beulah let out a cry of despair, watching her dog writhing in Tony's hold. "I was only looking after her, mister. I don't know you from Adam's house cat. You could be someone wanting to kill her, but as much as you want her, I don't think that's the case. I think it's something else."

"If what you've told me isn't the truth or if I have to come back here again, I'm gonna kill this dog and make you watch me while I do it," Tony threatened.

"Oh, please, mister, don't hurt him. I told you everything I know. There's nothing more I remember. Please don't hurt my baby."

Tony threw the dog at her. Shocked at the sight of her dog hurtling through the air toward her, Beulah responded at the last moment. She managed to catch him, trying to be as gentle as she could.

The dog writhed in her arms and worked its way up to her face to lick her chin. Beulah held him close as she thanked Tony repeatedly.

Tony waited for their reunion to be over. "If you go to the police or anybody, for that matter, and tell them about me being here, he's going to pay for it." He pointed at the dog.

Beulah held the animal close. "Don't worry, I won't tell nobody. Just please, don't hurt my baby." She kissed the dog all over his face.

Tony nodded at Mark, indicating it was time to leave.

Mark followed his boss, feeling disgusted at what Tony had done to the dog and the way he had treated Beulah, but overriding that was a feeling of great relief that he hadn't had to clean up another one of Tony's messes.

CHAPTER 30

▼

Garth came awake with a start, hearing Kendra's voice saying his name. "What? What's wrong?" he asked, on the verge of panic, thinking, Oh, shit, they're here.

Kendra climbed onto the bed, shivering violently. "Could I sleep in here with you? It's freezing in my room. I can't get warm."

He rubbed his face with his hands, noticed the coolness of the air against his bare arms, and was relieved it was only the cold air that drove her to his bed, not the evilness they anticipated.

"The wood stove must have gone out. I'll go get it started again." He sat up and noticed Kendra was wearing one of his thermal shirts, which hung down to mid thigh. "I was looking for that shirt yesterday," he groused.

Kendra ignored this as she climbed under the covers and curled up, shivering.

Garth swung his legs off the bed and sat there a moment. "Kendra, close your eyes."

She looked at him. "What?"

He glanced at her over his shoulders. "I don't have any clothes on. I need to get up to get dressed, so do me a favor and close your eyes for a minute."

She smiled. "You've seen what I've got. Why can't I see what you've got?"

"Keni," he growled.

"Oh, all right." She pulled his pillow over her head.

He rose, grabbed his fleece pants from the chair, and pulled them on. He turned and caught her watching.

"You got a nice butt for an old man, Fisher."

Garth couldn't see it but knew she was smiling. "What am I gonna do with you, Keni?" he growled.

She propped herself up on one elbow, studied him a moment, then said in a low voice, "Anything you want to, I guess."

Garth stopped moving and looked at her. "Are you flirting with me?"

"Is that what this is?"

He knew she was smiling by the tone of her voice.

"I'll be back in a minute," he said grouchily.

A few minutes later, Garth hurried into the bedroom and climbed under the covers, shivering himself. "The fire went out, but I got it going. It doesn't take long to heat this house, so your room should be warming up soon," he said, meaning, go to your room.

Kendra stayed put.

"You forget where it is?"

She had the comforter pulled up to beneath her mouth. "Please, Garth, let me stay here."

"No." He didn't want her that close, knowing what his body's response would be.

"Please. I'll stay over on my side of the bed. I won't get near you, if that's what you're worried about. Please let me stay. It's so warm here and so comfortable, and I don't want to have to go to that cold bed and try to get warm again."

He thought a minute, then said, in a grudging manner, "All right, just don't hog all the covers."

"Thanks." She sat up, leaned over, and kissed him on the corner of the mouth. "Thanks, Gar." She kissed the other side of his mouth. "Thanks, Gar." She kissed him fully on the lips, murmuring, "Thanks, Gar," against his mouth.

Garth drew his head back and regarded her. "You want to tell me what's going on?"

She looked caught.

He waited.

Kendra sat up and tucked her feet beneath her, gazing at him.

He remained silent.

She plucked at the comforter, watching the movement of her hands, then brought her eyes back to his.

He noticed the brimming tears and was surprised at this. "Kendra?"

"I'm trying to seduce you, I guess."

Garth sat up.

She wiped at her eyes. "I love you, Garth," she said, the words almost exploding out of her. "I love you with all my heart, but not only that, with my mind, as well. And since we kissed yesterday, I get this weird feeling in the pit of my stomach every time I look at you. And I've been thinking a lot about that, and I've come to the conclusion that maybe I need to love you physically." She looked him in the eyes. "No, there's no maybe to it. I want to love you with my body, Garth. I need to know. I have to know."

He reached out and touched her cheek with his finger, tracing down to her jaw line. "Know what?"

"Know that I can be a woman with you, know that I can love you fully, know that he hasn't killed that part of me." Her voice was low, furious.

"Ah, Keni." Garth reached for her and drew her against him.

"I want you to love me," she whispered, putting her mouth against his, "let me love you."

Afterward, while Garth was still joined with her, knowing full well she was not frigid; surprised, in fact, by the passion she had displayed, Kendra placed her hands on his face, looked into his eyes, her own glistening with the tears that were falling, and whispered, "I never dreamed it could feel like this, that it would be so intense, so beautiful, so mystical. Thank you, Garth. Thank you so much."

He kissed her welcome.

"How soon can we do that again?"

He laughed.

CHAPTER 31

▼

Tony called Vincent on his cell phone early the next morning. "Get over here now," he instructed, and hung up.

Without asking who, what, when, or where, Vincent drove to Tony's estate and headed straight to his office.

Tony was pacing excitedly as he talked into his cell phone. He gave his driver a deadly grin when he hesitated in the doorway and waved him inside.

Vincent noticed Mark was present, looking a little sick. He chose to ignore him, instead shuffled his cigarette pack out of his suit pocket and shook it, expelling a cigarette. He pulled it out, put it in his mouth, and replaced the pack, all the while listening to Tony on the phone. Shit, he thought, realizing Tony had traced the person who had given aid to Angel. Vincent worked at keeping his face expressionless.

Tony terminated the call and turned to Vincent. "Okay, we're flying to Houston."

"You found her?" Vincent asked, trying to keep his voice benign.

"No, but we found the truck driver who took her out of Knoxville." Tony smiled happily. "Looks like our luck's changing, buddy," he said grandly. "We're finally on her trail, it shouldn't be much longer now."

Vincent glanced at Mark, who cast his eyes away. "How'd you find the truck driver?"

"How the hell do you think?" Tony asked, his voice sarcastic. "I did what I wanted to, had Mark trail that waitress, then last night, me and him paid her a little visit." He glanced at Mark. "She was real cooperative."

Vincent stared at Tony, thinking, You dumb prick.

Tony brought his gaze back to him. "And no, I didn't kill the bitch, although I wanted to. Just found her weak spot, that's all. Her stupid dog of all things. Then all I had to do was help her appreciate the fact that that dumb animal would suffer mightily if she wasn't willing to help me."

"And I'm sure he did," Vincent said.

Tony shrugged. "A little. I was going to kill him, but then I thought, that's my bargaining point with her, you see, in case I need to go back, pay her another visit."

"So she told you about the truck driver," Vincent prodded.

"All she gave us was his first name, CB name, and the company he works for. But I know a man works for the DOT, he got on the phone and within an hour had all the information I needed. He even tracked him for us. You know those weigh stations can do that now? Said he last passed through one outside of Houston last night, so he called the company the guy works for. They have those computers in their trucks now; they track those drivers, too. He gave them some story or other about how the DOT needed to find him, and they located him right off the bat. I just got off the phone to some guys in Houston. They're gonna go pay him a visit, then take him someplace we can talk to him."

Vincent stubbed out his cigarette. "When's the plane leave?"

Tony grabbed his jacket. "Soon as we get to the airport."

After touching down in Houston, they were met on the tarmac by two men dressed completely in black with matching sunglasses on their faces and plenty of gold jewelry on their fingers. "And I thought the Mafia was dead," Vincent caustically remarked as they walked toward them.

The men directed their attention to Tony, huddling with him and conversing. They ignored Vincent and Mark, who stood beside Tony, constantly glancing around them, playing their part.

Tony finally turned to Vincent and motioned for him to draw closer as he moved away from the two men. Mark followed along behind.

"They got him in a warehouse, they're gonna take us there now," Tony said.

Vincent gave Tony a disbelieving look. "You're gonna ride in a car with those goons?"

Tony thought about that. "Yeah, you're right. That might not be such a good idea. We'll take our own car." He turned back to the two men. "My man wants to rent a car, so we'll follow you."

The men gave Tony a suspicious look, then shrugged synchronistically. "We'll meet you out front," the bigger one said, and they turned and left.

Vincent and Mark flanked Tony as they walked to the car rental counter. Tony explained to Vincent what he had been told by the men who met them: that they had gone to the truck stop where the truck driver had bedded down for the night, waited for him to exit his truck, then had snatched him. "He put up a fight, though," Tony said, glancing at Vincent. "They said they had to roughen him up a bit."

Vincent rolled his eyes.

"Well, what do you expect? We're not dealing with professionals here."

They rented a mid-sized sedan and followed the two men onto the interstate. Vincent drove with Tony beside him in the front passenger seat and Mark sitting in back.

"Should have known they'd be driving a black car," Vincent said, falling in behind them.

They arrived at the warehouse about twenty minutes later and stood outside, studying the exterior, which was covered with grime and graffiti. The windows were boarded over and the roll-up doors on the loading docks had iron grills across their fronts.

Tony looked at the other two men and raised his eyebrows. They didn't respond as they walked toward a door in the side, which was unlocked.

Tony, Vincent, and Mark followed the men down a dusty hallway to a room near the end. The door was open, the inside dimly lit by an overhead florescent tube which flickered dimly with a strobe-like effect.

I'm gonna get a migraine, we have to stay in here very long, Vincent thought, stepping inside. He directed his attention to the man sitting in a chair, his arms behind him, hands and feet bound. Vincent was surprised to see Luke was a tall and angularly built black man who looked to be in his mid thirties. He had half-expected a middle-aged white guy with a potbelly and missing teeth. At least, that was Vincent's idea of a truck driver.

Tony stepped into the room, studied the man a moment, then turned to the two strangers. "Thanks for your help," he said in a gruff voice and waited for them to leave.

Vincent watched the man, whose eyes flickered angrily from Tony to Vincent to Mark. He remained mute, though. Vincent supposed that was a learned lesson from the bruises and contusions over his face.

After the men had exited, Tony gently closed the door, then approached Luke. He opened his suit coat to show the gun holstered beneath his right arm.

The man's eyes widened slightly, but he didn't say anything.

Tony stood in front of Luke. "Now, we can make this easy or we can make this hard, your choice."

Luke gave Tony a surly look. "Mister, I ain't done nothing to you, so I don't see that we got anything to talk about."

Tony reached into his coat pocket, pulled out the picture of Angel, and threw it down on the table beside the black man.

Luke glanced at it, then back to Tony, his face noncommittal.

"You picked her up outside of Knoxville, Tennessee, back in November," Tony said, his voice low, almost soft. "All I want from you is where you took her."

Luke's eyes narrowed. "You got the wrong man," he said, his voice matching Tony's. "I ain't never seen that girl. Shoot, I'd be a stupid idiot to be driving around the South with a white woman in my truck."

Tony backhanded him.

The man's face was slung to the right from the force. He let it stay there a moment, then brought it around to stare sullenly at Tony once more.

Tony noticed the detritus littering the table and turned his attention to that.

Vincent surmised the goons had emptied the guy's pockets, as he watched Tony shuffle keys, loose change, and a Chapstick around, then pick up a worn, brown leather wallet.

Luke watched Tony closely.

Tony opened the wallet, pulled out some bills, and threw them on the table. He continued to riffle through it, until his fingers paused and his face changed from a scowl to a smile. "Well, well, what do we have here?" he asked no one, pulling out a picture of two young children.

Vincent stepped closer, saw a small boy and girl who looked to be twins in the picture, in front of what appeared to be a merry-go-round, both with little hats on their heads and big grins on their faces.

Tony pulled Luke's driver's license from the wallet, studied it, then focused his attention on the truck driver. "These little rugrats have got to be yours, they look too much like you not to be." Tony put the picture down on the table.

Luke's face now wore a sick, worried look.

"Okay, let me put this to you in a way you can understand." Tony sat on the table sideways, one foot resting on the floor, one dangling. "You don't tell me what I want to know, I'm gonna have my man here," and at this point, he turned and glanced at Vincent, "go to the address on this driver's license, pay a little visit there, see who he can see, what he can find—"

"They ain't there," Luke interrupted. "And you can kill me if you want, but I'll never tell you where my kids are."

"You didn't let me finish," Tony said, his voice mild. "If they're not there, why, I guess I'll just put the guys to work who found you. They'll find them. Until then, looks like this is gonna be your home. And once they get them, I'm gonna have my man bring them here, and you're gonna watch them die, slowly and painfully."

Luke glared at Tony.

Vincent could see him straining against the ropes that bound him, could almost hear what the man was thinking in his head, that all he wanted was to get out of that chair and get his hands on Tony. Vincent half-wished he would get free.

"Unless, of course," Tony continued, "you want to tell me where you took her."

Luke remained mute.

Tony turned to Vincent. "Go," he said in a low voice.

"No, wait," Luke said, when Vincent got to the door.

Vincent turned back.

Sweat was beading on Luke's forehead and upper lip and his jaw was working. "I'll tell you, man, just promise you'll leave my kids alone. They're innocent, they haven't done a blessed thing."

"You tell me what I want to know, nobody gets hurt," Tony said.

Luke looked relieved. "Okay. I picked her up at this truck stop north of Knoxville. She looked to be in pretty bad shape. No coat, it was freezing outside, acting like she was in pain. She said she was needing a ride anywhere. Man, I could tell she was in trouble but I didn't ask and she didn't tell. So, I told her I was heading to Eastern North Carolina to pick up some Christmas trees and I could take her that far, and she said yeah, she'd like to go."

Luke stopped talking and gave Tony a pleading look.

Tony stood. "And?"

"She was sick, man, weak. I was wondering if maybe I shouldn't take her to a hospital. So I stopped at this truck stop outside of Black Mountain, North Carolina to get her some hot chocolate and something for her stomach. She said she was having a little pain, but man, I could tell, she was in a lot of pain. But when I got back out to the truck, she was gone. I searched for her for over an hour and couldn't find her anywhere, so I figured she must have hooked up with another driver and gone on. I got to tell you, mister, I worried about that girl some. She wasn't in good health, I don't think." His face then became hopeful. "Is that why you're trying to find her, so you can help her with whatever was wrong with her?"

"Yeah," Tony said, "I want to help her."

Luke nodded.

"That's the last you saw of her?" Tony asked.

"Yeah. I've worried some about her, though. She was a real nice woman, real sweet. Had this kind of calm air about her, made me feel peaceful just knowing her."

Vincent found himself mentally nodding in agreement.

Tony turned to him. "I'm gonna go out to the car, make some calls, get our people headed over to Black Mountain. You want to handle this or you still got a problem with that?" He cast his head in the direction of Luke.

Vincent, knowing he had to get back in Tony's good graces long enough to find Angel, nodded. "I'll handle it."

Tony left.

Mark shifted uneasily.

Luke was watching Vincent. "You're gonna kill me, ain't you, even though I tried to help that poor girl?"

"It's not my decision." Vincent unbuttoned his coat, reached into the holster, and pulled out his gun, staring at Luke, who was now sweating profusely.

Vincent glanced at Mark. "Go out there, tell Tony before he sends any of our guys over there, he might want to use that guy we used a few years ago, that tracker goes by the name of Mountain Man. He knows that area like the back of his hand."

Mark nodded with a look of relief and left.

Vincent approached the man, laid his gun on the table, reached into his pants pocket, and pulled out a switchblade. He exposed the blade, then leaned down close to Luke to place the knife at his throat, just in case Tony wandered back in. He spoke barely above a whisper. "I'm not gonna kill you. You saved her and I owe you for that. So what I'm gonna do is put this knife in your hand so you can cut those ropes once I'm out of here, all right? But give us ten minutes to clear out. I don't want Tony to see you come running out of that building, us still in the lot. Then he'd kill you and me both."

Luke nodded, relieved.

Vincent straightened, glanced toward the door, then stepped around to Luke's back and placed the knife in his open palm. He picked up his gun from the table, placed it close to Luke's head, and pulled the trigger.

Luke cried out.

Vincent shot the gun again, eliciting another cry of alarm from Luke. "Just in case somebody's close by listening." He replaced the gun back in his shoulder holster.

"Man, you got to watch that guy if he finds her," Luke whispered, nodding in the direction of the door, meaning Tony. "I don't like the look in his eyes. I'm scared for her, he finds her."

Vincent studied Luke for a minute. "Me, too, buddy, me, too." He walked toward the door.

"You'll protect her?" Luke asked, not letting it go.

Vincent stopped, turned, and looked at him. "I'll see to it he doesn't hurt her. You can count on it."

"Hey mister?"

"Yeah."

"She left two hundred dollars laying on the seat of my cab. I got it in my wallet there. You mind returning it to her when you find her?"

Vincent thought, *That sounds like something Angel would do.* "You keep it. Lord knows, you earned it." He turned to leave, then glanced back. "After we've cleared out, you might want to consider working for another trucking company or at least getting your route changed, make sure you don't get identified by those goons that found you."

"I've been thinking about moving further West. I guess that decision just got made for me."

Vincent nodded in agreement, then left.

Mark was waiting outside the building, his face ashen. "Get in the car," Vincent told him, then climbed behind the wheel.

Tony was on the phone, talking to the bounty hunter they had used before, the one that called himself the Mountain Man, the one Vincent thought was an idiot.

Tony was telling him he was sending a picture to him, wanted him to go to Black Mountain, North Carolina, and as discretely as he could, ask around, see if anyone had seen the woman in the picture.

"You know how to talk to those people?" Tony asked, as if the denizens of that area were a different breed.

Tony nodded at the assurance he was being given. "Whatever you do, don't get made, don't ask the wrong person. We lose her because you get stupid, I'm coming after you, and I'm not kidding. I want to find this woman and I don't want her scared off."

Tony glanced at Vincent, who lifted his eyebrows, and answered his unspoken question with another nod.

Vincent started the car and left the lot, watching in the rear-view mirror, making sure Luke didn't make a sudden appearance. He breathed a sight of relief once they turned onto the interstate.

C H A P T E R   32

▼

Vincent was worried about the Mountain Man. Even though the guy was an idiot, if Angel was still in Black Mountain, there was a chance he could find her, and Vincent didn't want this man to find her.

The next morning, he sat smoking in Tony's office, mulling the situation over, half-listening to Tony talking to his tracker, ascertaining he had received the email with Angel's picture attached and was hot on the trail.

After Tony hung up, Vincent stubbed out his cigarette. "I want to go help," he said, giving Tony an intent look.

Tony drew back, surprised.

"Look, Tony, I feel responsible for Angel running off like she did, and I want to be involved in this. You don't need me here. You got all kinds of guys can drive you around, watch you throw your temper-tantrums."

Tony glared.

"I don't trust this guy, okay? Sure, he's helped us before and got the job done, but I'd feel better if I was there right alongside him, trying to find her. That way we'd both know, once we have her, she won't get away again and nothing will happen to her."

Tony thought about this, fully aware of the Mountain Man's tendency to rape women, his out-of-control behavior at times. He was known for killing a man he had been hired to find, simply because the man made a rude comment about his manner of dress.

"I'll leave today, meet up with him this afternoon. I'll call you every day, let you know what's going on."

Tony liked having Vincent around. Although he never told him or anyone else this, Vincent was the only man among his subordinates he actually trusted. He finally sighed, knowing it would be better to have one of his men in on the search, and the only one he had faith in protecting his Angel would be Vinnie. "Okay, do it. Call me when you get there. Don't make me have to try to find you."

Vincent stood. "Call him back, tell him to meet me at that truck stop the driver lost Angel at today at two. That'll give me enough time."

Tony picked up the phone.

When Vincent arrived at the truck stop/restaurant, he spotted Mountain Man sitting at the counter, eating lunch. "Mountain Man," he said, taking the seat next to him, hiding his amusement at the buckskin jacket and Daniel Boone-style cap the man always wore, thinking again, What an idiot. He wondered if the man knew how stupid it was to go around calling himself Mountain Man, never giving his Christian name.

The tracker grunted his way.

Vincent pulled out his cigarette pack. "What's wrong, you ain't happy to see me?"

"I don't need no babysitter when I'm tracking," Mountain Man said.

Vincent turned away from the sight of mushed up food in the man's mouth. "Yeah, well, the woman you're tracking is probably the most valuable thing you'll ever find, and I'm here to make sure nothing happens to her."

Mountain Man cast him a baleful look.

"Shouldn't have killed that guy 'cause he didn't like the way you dress," Vincent said, taking pokes.

Mountain Man ignored him.

"You got anything yet?"

"Nah. Just got started this morning. I figured I'd go around to some of the businesses in Black Mountain, stores and such, show her picture, tell 'em she's my daughter or something, see what develops."

"You need my help with that?"

Mountain Man gave Vincent a critical look. "Hell, son, you'd stick out like a sore thumb. People around here don't cater to Yankees."

Vincent shrugged, as if that didn't bother him, and took a final drag from his cigarette. "But they cater to you, I take it?" He deliberately blew smoke in the man's direction.

Mountain Man watched him, gauging his sincerity. "They're my kind of people."

Vincent thought only perverts were this guy's kind of people. He ground out his cigarette in the aluminum ashtray provided for customers, then stood. "I'll be in the area. Call me when you get done or if anything develops while you're checking around." He fished in his jacket, found a business card, and placed it on the bar in front of the tracker. "My cell phone number's on there."

Mountain Man glanced at the card, then back to his food.

Vincent leaned down close to the man but drew back a little at the odor of an unwashed body. "You don't keep me in the loop, Mountain Man," he said, his voice low, "I'm on the phone to Tony. And you know you don't want to mess with the man, unless you got a death wish going on I don't know about."

Mountain Man reached out, plucked the card off the countertop, and put it in his pocket.

"I expect a report by four." Vincent adjusted his sport coat and left without waiting for a reply.

Vincent drove through the streets of downtown Black Mountain, studying the businesses, thinking how much he liked this pretty little town. He hoped Angel was still in the area so he could help her to get away. He had been disappointed she hadn't called him for further aid, but had not been surprised by this, either. After all, he worked for her husband.

Vincent finally found what he was looking for, parked in the small lot provided for customers, and climbed out of the car. He stepped inside a country store that looked like it would have belonged there 100 years earlier, but not in the present.

Vincent stood just inside the doorway and took off his sunglasses, letting his eyes adjust to the dimness of the store, glancing around. He finally spotted who he thought was either the manager or owner, a rangy man who looked to be in his 70's, sporting white hair and a white moustache, with stooped shoulders and a small potbelly resting between his black suspenders. The man was watching Vincent with suspicion bordering on hostility.

Vincent walked over to him, fished in his coat pocket for a picture of Angel, and brought it out to show to him. "I'm looking for this woman. You seen her around here?" He was glad at the reaction he got from the man, which was what he had been hoping for, knowing if Angel were still here, she'd be warned fairly shortly.

CHAPTER 33

▼

Their days seemed to be lost in a haze of hastily doing chores, checking their perimeter alarms, eating and cleaning and taking care of hygiene interspersed with furious, fulminative lovemaking; long, leisurely lovemaking; playful, fun lovemaking; intense, passionate lovemaking; and friendly, comfortable lovemaking.

Boo and Sarge seemed to become disgusted with these two and chose to stay in the sunroom most of the time, away from all the activity going on between the only two-legged animals in the house.

Kendra had decided she now liked sex just fine and wanted to explore each and every aspect. Garth was more than happy to go along with whatever she wished to revel in. They had spent the morning in bed, indulging in what Kendra had come to term one of their sexual marathons, each act seeming to blend into another one, never culminating to an end until they were both to the point of either let it go or die, coming together with a force uplifting, shattering, and a little frightening. They lay entwined afterwards, breathing raspily, sweat drying, body fluids leaking, coming down.

The kitchen door banged open and Thad yelled, "Anybody in here?" startling them both.

Garth shot out of bed, grabbed his boxers, and put them on at a run, half-afraid Thad would come barreling down the hall and into the bedroom, catching Kendra there. Garth wasn't sure if she was ready to own up to this yet or not. He rushed into the kitchen, sweat glistening on his body, his face red, his voice still rough. "Hey!" he said, looking as guilty as sin. He watched Thad put down a bag of something or other on the counter.

Thad took the time to study him, then nodded and said, "Uh-huh."

"What?" Garth asked, trying to appear innocent.

Kendra entered the kitchen wearing a tank top and pair of Garth's sweatpants, rolled at the waist to reveal a lovely navel.

Garth fought the urge to put his tongue there.

"Hey!" she said to Thad, her flushed face glowing.

He repeated the "Uh-huh" bit.

She gave him an innocent look. "What?"

Thad stared at them.

Kendra finally gave a sigh, moved to stand by Garth, wrapped her arms around him, lay her head against his shoulder, and simply said, "Uh-huh."

Thad frowned.

Kendra pulled away from Garth and approached Thad. She reached up on tiptoe and gave him a kiss on the cheek, bringing a smile to his face. She put her arms around him and hugged him. "Well?" she asked, looking up.

"I've been wondering if you two were ever going to get around to that," he growled.

Kendra smiled and kissed him on the cheek once more, then returned to Garth and gave him a more passionate kiss on the lips.

They stood, arms wrapped around each other, watching Thad watching them.

Kendra finally straightened somewhat as she studied their friend. "There's something you need to tell us."

Garth looked more sharply at Thad, then back to Kendra, wondering how in the hell she could read that on his face.

Thad seemed to be searching for a way to answer her.

"He's here," Kendra said, her voice rising.

"No, no," Thad said, trying to waylay the panic he saw on her face.

Garth protectively drew Kendra tighter against him. "What is it?"

"One of his goons, is that the word you use, Keni, was over at Mert's store this morning, showing your picture around, asking if anybody'd seen you."

"How the hell could they have tracked her here?" Garth asked, his voice rising angrily.

"I don't know that they have. Maybe they're just hitting all small towns in this area. Who knows?"

Kendra was wildly wondering if anyone had spotted her with Garth. "What did Mert tell him?"

"Told him to get his Yankee ass out of his store and not come around asking about nobody or nothing." Thad grinned. "Told him we were mountain folks and we didn't cotton to any strangers coming into our midst. That even if he had seen anyone looked like that pretty young thing in the picture, which he hadn't, he wouldn't tell a damn Yankee."

Kendra smiled uneasily, then sobered, reading Thad's expression. "What else?"

Garth gave her another look.

"Well, you don't know Mert, but he's got this sort of offhanded way of asking about things, and in a roundabout way, he let me know he thinks Garth has a woman up here."

"Damnit!" Garth exploded.

"I took care of it, though."

"How?" Kendra asked.

Thad grinned. "Got mad, acted like I was jealous, told ole Mert Garth and I had a thing going and he better not betray me and have one of those up here."

Kendra burst out laughing.

"Very funny," Garth said, then added a little worriedly, "You think Mert bought it?"

Thad shrugged. "Whether he did or didn't, it doesn't matter. He meant what he told that goon. We protect our own up here. He won't say anything."

"What makes him think I've got somebody up here?" Garth wondered, like Kendra, if anyone had spotted her. They had been so careful.

"Well, you have been seen purchasing such items as feminine hygiene products, panties, scented shampoo, body shampoo…"

"Okay already. But I thought I explained about the, well, feminine hygiene products and underwear. You said it sounded legit to you," Garth accused Thad.

"Yeah, and I made it sound legit to Mert," Thad said in an affable way. "Convincing him about the other stuff was a little harder."

Kendra smiled. "What'd you tell him?"

"Told him I needed my honey to smell good," Thad said, grinning.

Kendra laughed delightedly at this.

Garth frowned copiously. "I don't know if I want people on this mountain thinking I'm gay," he observed, more to himself than anyone else.

"Oh, darlin', you are most definitely not gay." Kendra put her arms around him and gave him a lecherous look, then turned back to Thad. "You think he believes you?"

Thad considered this. "Well, Garth hasn't had a woman up here that I know of…" he gave Garth a curious glance "…since he moved back. People have mentioned that fact from time to time, and maybe that's been in the back of their minds, you know, wondering which way he swings. Plus the fact that he's good friends with me, the only gay person on this mountain, well, seems logical, don't you think?"

Kendra laughed long at this.

Garth gave her an irritated look.

"Honey, after this is over, I promise I'll make it well known that you are the most ungay man I have ever in my life known."

"I'll hold you to that," Garth growled. He glanced at the bag Thad had placed on the bar. "What's that?"

Thad smiled widely. "Oh! Mert recommended I buy this for you, says you'll smell so good you'll be irresistible." He pulled out a bottle of scented bath oil.

"Shit fire!" Garth exploded, causing Thad and Kendra to laugh.

CHAPTER 34

▼

It was pure coincidence Mountain Man found Kendra and only because he happened to be in the right place at the right time; or in Kendra's case, the wrong place. The tracker had gotten tired of the Yankee gangster trailing along behind him, questioning his every move, pushing him, not treating him with the proper respect he felt he deserved. He decided to take a break early one morning and do a little illegal hunting. He would go deep into the Black Mountains range, where a game warden wouldn't be so prone to be, especially at this time of day, and see if he could shoot himself a buck. He could sell the head and antlers for a fair price in Gatlinburg, Tennessee.

Mountain Man set off before daybreak, knowing Vincent wouldn't expect him to check in for a few hours yet, wearing his standard uniform of buckskin trousers, jacket, and coon hat, with his rifle thrown over his shoulder. He climbed an old mountain trail he knew about, heading toward the top, wishing he'd never agreed to this job. Tony Salvatori was the only man who instilled fear in Mountain Man, knowing the man's reputation for killing for no legitimate reason at all. The tracker was beginning to panic now, thinking he'd probably end up dead if he didn't find this woman and find her soon. He was feeling out of sorts, aware that people around this area viewed him with suspicion, did not trust him, and he blamed Vincent for this.

Mountain Man began following a small stream. The going was rough in some areas, but he was enjoying this outing, the chance to stretch his legs, walk among the wildlife, exist in the environment he felt he belonged; thinking he had been born in the wrong century.

Close to the top of the mountain, the tracker heard a horse's hooves trotting toward him and stepped off the dirt path he had been following into an area packed thick with wild rhododendron bushes. He hid behind the thicket, hoping it wasn't a game warden who would be curious as to what he was doing on this mountain with a rifle.

The horse slowed to a walk and continued on. Mountain Man peered between the branches and caught sight of a woman riding an American Saddle Horse bareback, no reins of any kind. He respected any woman who would ride a horse in this manner, especially an American Saddle, with their propensity to be high-strung and startle easily. Even from a distance, the woman was a looker, and he debated getting her off that horse and having his way with her. He finally decided he'd better behave with Salvatori's man in the area.

The tracker watched the woman coming toward him and it wasn't until she was close enough that he could have jumped out and yelled "Boo!" startling the horse and sending it running, before he realized who was astride the animal.

Mountain Man moved to lunge out of the bushes so he could grab her, take her into custody, then back to Vincent, but hesitated. Vincent had repeatedly drilled the message into him that if he saw her, not to approach her, just let him know where she was, and he'd take it from there.

Mountain Man gave the woman a chance to get far enough away from him that she wouldn't see him if she looked back, then began to follow the trail left by the horse, which the animal made easy enough with his droppings and hoof prints.

As he tracked Kendra, Mountain Man thought about this situation and came upon an idea to get into Tony Salvatori's good graces and not have to deal with his moron Vincent. He'd simply trail her to where she was hiding out, then go back to his jeep and call Tony directly. He would give him the excuse that he couldn't find Vincent to tell him and wanted Tony to hear the news as quickly as possible.

The woman rode the horse almost to the top of the mountain. She turned onto a narrow drive lined with sun-bleached river rock and shadowed by trees running along each side. The lane ended at a large clearing, in the center of which sat a handsome, log-cabin home featuring an expansive, wooden, wraparound deck. Smoke trailed lazily from the chimney and the sun shone brightly on the forest-green, metal roof. A man was standing on the front porch, watching the woman travel toward him. He held a mug in one hand and waved to her with the other. A large, bluish-gray dog bounded toward the horse, barking with excitement. The woman used her feet to nudge the horse into a trot and rode into the yard, then around the house to what appeared to be a large barn. She stopped the horse outside a fenced pasture, slid off the animal, shooed the horse inside, and closed the gate. She stooped to pet the dog, then rose as the man joined her, threw her arms around him, and kissed him on the lips.

Mountain Man raised his eyebrows at that. He watched as the man and woman continued to embrace, feeling their passion from where he stood, then, arms around each other's waists, walked into the house. The woman's laugher reached him, reminding him of a long-lost memory from his childhood.

Traveling down the mountain, the tracker thought about the situation. He wondered how Tony's wife had come to be here and who was the man she was with? When he told Tony, should he tell him about the man? He was well aware of Tony's temper and was afraid that, being the barer of bad news, he might have to endure Tony's violent nature. Men had been known to die for bringing Tony news he did not wish to hear.

By the time Mountain Man reached the road and climbed into his jeep, he had decided the best course of action would be to tell Tony where she was but not that she was with anyone. Tell him he saw her riding a horse and go inside the house. When Tony showed up, draw him a map, tell him he had another job to do, collect his money, and get gone before Tony got up the mountain and found something he wouldn't like. And maybe, if God were taking care of things, Tony would be the one who would end up dead and not the man who was with Angel. Mountain Man was certain that one of them would not be breathing by the time it was over.

CHAPTER 35

▼

Each morning at nine, Vincent and Mountain Man met at a local country restaurant for breakfast, during which Vincent would grill the tracker about what he had planned for that day. As Vincent sat, waiting, he decided he needed to kill Mountain Man and do it soon. Although the man's efforts to locate Angel had not been fruitious, Vincent knew it was only a matter of time before Mountain Man found someone who could provide him with information as to her whereabouts.

Vincent had wanted to murder the tracker since before he actually came to Black Mountain, but had decided it might be best to allow him to find Angel, then kill him, dispose of the body, and convince Angel to leave the area. Vincent knew ways she could disappear and never be found, not even by Tony and the countless thugs he had at his disposal.

Now Vincent had changed his mind, knowing enough time had elapsed that Tony would be convinced they had seriously tried to locate his missing wife. And when Mountain Man came up missing, Vincent would simply tell Tony the man was terrified Tony was getting impatient and had taken off, afraid of Tony's temper.

As for Angel, he would tell Tony he had a lead he was investigating that hopefully would lead him to her, then would divert Tony's attention to another part of the country. He would pay a visit once more to the old man in the grocery store and leave a final message for Angel.

When nine-thirty rolled around, Vincent began thinking he might be lucky, maybe the guy had decided on his own that it was time to leave the area. He picked up his cell with the intention of calling Tony to report that their tracker may have gone missing.

Tony answered immediately. Vincent could tell by the staticky sound issuing from the handset that his boss was in a car that was moving.

Before Vincent could say anything, Tony said, "You seen Mountain Man yet?"

"No. That's why I was calling."

"Well, he found Angel this morning. I'm headed that way now. I should be there in an hour at the most. I want you to—"

"Wait a minute! He found her? Why didn't he tell me? Where the hell is he anyway?"

"He told me he couldn't find you, so he called me instead," Tony said in an accusing tone.

Vincent considered this, knowing that was pure fabrication on the tracker's part. "He's lying, Tony. I've been right by my cell phone."

"Well, whether he is or not, I don't give a damn at this point. The thing is, he found Angel. He said he'll take us to her as soon as I get there."

Vincent was furious. "Where is he?" he asked, trying to keep his tone calm.

"Hell if I know. We're supposed to meet him at that truck stop you met him at the other day. We'll be there by eleven."

"I'll see you there." Vincent terminated the call and rose, throwing ones down on the table. He left to track down Mountain Man before Tony got there.

Vincent drove straight to the truck stop and parked on the outskirts of the parking lot. He walked around, checking cars, looking for Mountain Man's jeep. Not finding it, he went inside to search for the man, cursing to himself. He was worried the tracker had made him and had figured out he wanted to get to Angel before her husband did.

Vincent stepped outside and searched the parking lot once more, knowing in his gut the man had pulled one over on him, wondering why he had gone over his head.

When Tony's SUV pulled into the lot, Vincent strode toward the vehicle and waited for Tony to exit. He noted his boss had brought with him an anxious looking Mark as well as Anson, another one of Angel's bodyguards. He felt dread in his heart as he watched a third man exit the car: Jamille, a former football player for the University of Tennessee who had quickly developed a liking for killing. Vincent hated this young man, hated the crazed look in his eyes, his macabre sense of humor.

Tony stepped out of the SUV behind the other three and joined Vincent. "Where's Mountain Man?"

Vincent shrugged. "I've been looking for him myself. I came here straight after I talked to you."

Tony turned and nodded in the direction of Mark, Anson, and Jamille, who headed for the store/restaurant combination that sat in the middle of the huge parking area.

Vincent pulled out a cigarette and tried to act nonchalant. "He tell you where Angel is?"

Tony shook his head as he looked around. "You trust this guy?"

Vincent lit up and took a drag, then shook his head. "He's too weird, Tony, too involved in living his Daniel Boone fantasy."

Tony nodded, then his eyes fixated on something beyond Vincent's shoulder.

Vincent turned around. Mountain Man was walking toward them. "Where the hell have you been?" Vincent raged at him, barely resisting the urge to strike the man down.

Mountain Man ignored him.

"I could have already been wherever you found her and brought her back here for Tony," Vincent said, glancing at his boss.

Mountain Man approached Tony and handed him a piece of paper. "I drew you up a map. It's easy enough to find the house she's staying at. Just follow the directions on there, it'll lead you right to her."

Tony took the paper and studied it briefly, then brought his eyes to the tracker. "I thought you were gonna go with us, show us how to get up there."

Mountain Man cleared his throat.

Vincent knew then that the man was afraid and wondered what exactly he had found.

"I just got off the phone with another client who's hired me to start tracking a girl down in South Carolina. Wants me to leave right away. I figured I'd go over them directions with you, make sure you know how to get there, collect my money, then I'm on my way. You don't need me for what's gonna go down once you find her."

"What do you mean, gonna go down?" Vincent snarled.

The man shrugged. "Just, I don't want to know why you want her, what you want to do with her. It ain't none of my business. And the less I know, the less I can tell the police if anyone comes looking for me, seeing as I was the one trying to find the woman."

"How'd you find her?" Vincent asked.

"I was out early this morning, stalking a buck on top of one of these mountain ranges and caught sight of her riding a horse. I trailed her to a house, a log cabin practically sitting on top of the mountain, and waited till she went inside. When I came back down, I couldn't reach you, so called Mr. Salvatori here."

"You never tried to reach me," Vincent said, "so don't lie about it."

Mountain Man ignored him.

"She with anybody?" Tony asked.

Mountain Man's eyes slid away and Vincent knew why the man wanted to leave. He was fearful of Tony knowing what he had found. Vincent was afraid for Angel if she had been taken in by another man.

"When I seen her, she was by herself," the tracker replied, bringing his eyes back to Tony's.

Tony spread the map out on the hood of the SUV. "Okay, go over these directions with me."

Vincent stood, lost in thought, trying to devise a way to get to Angel before her husband.

Tony interrupted by saying, "Vinnie, you're good at directions. Come over here and listen to how we need to get up there."

Vincent joined them. "Don't let him leave, Tony." He watched the fear come into the tracker's eyes.

"I done my job. Ain't no need for me to stay around," Mountain Man said.

Vncent ignored him. "Like I said earlier, if he had tried to reach me, he would have, but he didn't for some reason. Now what if she's gotten away in the meantime? There was at least an hour and a half window there for her to do that."

The tracker's face grew red. "I said I tried to reach you. You never answered."

Vincent pulled out his cell phone, keyed in the menu, then calls received within the last twenty-four hours. None were from Mountain Man. He showed this to Tony.

Tony turned to the tracker and gave him a suspicious look.

"I ain't gonna go up there with you," the man said. "I ain't gonna get pulled into something involving you, Mr. Salvatori. No offense, but I know what kind of reputation you got. Any killing's gonna go down, I'd just as soon stay out of it."

"You're going," Tony said, his voice low, his eyes glistening. "She isn't up there and you lost her, you're gonna pay for it."

Mark, Anson, and Jamille had joined them and, hearing this, loosely encircled Mountain Man in case he tried to run.

"Get in the car," Tony said to the tracker.

Mountain Man reluctantly approached the SUV and waited for Mark to open the door to the back seat. He climbed in, followed by Mark. Jamille walked around, got in on the other side and sat by the window. The tracker was now sandwiched between the two bodyguards. Anson took the seat in the rear and positioned himself directly behind Mountain Man.

Vincent got behind the wheel. "Okay, now you can show us," he said to Mountain Man, watching him in the rear-view mirror, seeing hatred shining in his eyes.

At the foot of the road that would take them to the house, Tony told Vincent to pull over and stop. They stared at an iron gate barring their entrance onto the graveled lane. "How isolated is this place?" Tony asked Mountain Man.

"It's isolated where it sits, but there's houses scattered all over this mountain.

"So someone could warn them if they see us coming."

"Yeah, could be."

Tony thought a minute. "We better go in on foot."

"I ain't going up there," Mountain Man said. "You can shoot me if you want, but I ain't gonna be part of whatever you got planned for that girl."

Tony could see the man meant what he said. "Tell me the quickest way to get up this mountain to the house."

Mountain Man told them about the trail he had found, which branched off from the road about 100 yards away.

"Vinnie, stay here with this piece of garbage. I'll deal with him when I get back." Tony opened the door, but before exiting turned back to him. "Pull the car into that clearing as far as it'll go, try to make it as near invisible as you can, then wait for us to get back here."

Vincent wanted to go with them and started to protest, but then thought better of it. "Sure thing, boss." He watched Tony, Mark, Jamille, and Anson exit the car, climb over the gate and head up the lane toward the foot trail.

After they were out of sight, Vincent turned back to the tracker. "Okay, what'd you find that's got you so scared?"

The man gave him a belligerent look.

"Tell me and I'll let you go. If you don't tell me, I'll keep you here for Tony when he gets back. And believe me, I can tell, what he's got planned for you ain't gonna be pretty."

Mountain Man's eyes brightened, then returned to the dull pallor they usually were. "I saw this woman go up to the house and there was a man there waiting on her. I seen them kissing. Looked to me like she was real happy being there with him."

Vincent became alarmed. Tony would kill them both if he caught them together.

"Anything else you can tell me, like another way up that mountain?"

"Way I sent them's the best way on foot. Other than that, you'd have to use that lane and it'll take you longer to get there."

"You want to live, I'd suggest you hightail it out of here now. Don't let Tony catch you when he comes back."

Without saying a word, Mountain Man opened the door and had disappeared by the time Vincent turned around to see which direction he had gone.

Vincent pulled the car into the clearing as far as he could get it, shot out of the car, and headed up the mountain at a run.

CHAPTER 36

▼

Garth had a breakfast of fresh strawberries, warm biscuits and honey waiting on Kendra when she returned from her early-morning ride. Afterwards, they retired to the bedroom at Kendra's suggestion. She took the jar of honey with her, a gleam in her eyes. Garth, knowing what was coming, grinned madly, anxious to get there and get started.

They did chores together afterward, then Kendra saddled up the gelding she usually rode, wanting to take a longer ride. Garth told her he would catch up to her when he finished chopping kindling.

"Where's Boo?" Kendra asked, looking around.

"Took off after some scent he caught," Garth said, retying her saddlebags.

Kendra looked concerned.

"Don't worry. He never goes far. I'll bring him with me when I come."

She gave him a lingering kiss, then left.

Garth was saddling his horse, envisioning leading Kendra to the clearing, making love to her there by the stream, followed by skinny-dipping, when he heard a shot, followed almost immediately by a horse squealing with pain. He stiffened and his eyes darted anxiously, trying to discern which direction the noises had come from. He froze at the sound of a woman's keening overriding the horse's sounds of agony. Kendra! he thought. He grabbed his gun from the holster hanging from the barn door, tucked it into the back of his jeans, and ran into the woods.

Within seconds, the horse's squealing began to weaken, then stop altogether. If not for Kendra's sounds of grief, Garth would have been unable to track where they were. He finally came upon her in the clearing, the very one where he had wanted to make love to her. His eyes landed on the horse on the ground, dying from a bullet wound, he was sure. Kendra was draped over the animal, sobbing into its neck. Garth squelched the mingling feelings of grief and panic that threatened to overtake him and forced himself to slow down before he entered the clearing in order to scan the area. Three men were standing around, all viewing the scene impassively as if watching a movie.

Garth stepped into the clearing and raised his gun, using both hands. "Get away from her!" he yelled forcefully.

The three men turned to him. A moment too late, Garth noticed their eyes shift to his left. He began to bring his arms around, then felt the pressure of a gun at his temple, stopping his movements.

One of the men in the clearing who was tall, powerfully built, and dark-headed, and who Garth immediately recognized as Tony Salvatori, stepped toward him.

Everyone's attention was on Garth and no one noticed that Kendra had stopped wailing at the sound of Garth's voice and was now stealthily reaching into her saddlebags with one hand, wiping her eyes with the other.

"Kill him," Tony commanded the man beside Garth, almost immediately startling at the sound of a gun going off behind him.

They all turned to see Kendra holding a smoking gun in the air, then watched as she slowly brought it to her own temple.

Tony held his hand out toward the man beside Garth, signaling him to wait.

"Keni, don't!" Garth yelled.

Holding the gun to her head, Kendra's eyes boring into Tony's, she said, her voice shaky, "You hurt him, I'll kill myself."

"That so?" Tony asked, as if he found this amusing.

"I so much as hear the sound of a bullet being chambered or see his finger move one fraction of an inch, I'll pull this trigger, take me away from you forever."

Tony studied her for a moment, then chortled derisively, aware of her previous fear of firearms. "What's this, my Angel knows how to use a gun now? I thought you hated weapons of any kind."

Kendra cocked the gun, alternately staring at Tony and the man beside Garth.

Tony grew serious. "You trying to tell me you got feelings for this guy?" he asked her with disbelief.

"He saved my life, Tony. I owe him." She glanced toward Garth. "You ought to thank him for saving your wife."

Tony studied Garth, then said, a gleam in his eyes, "Well, then, I owe you my deepest gratitude."

Garth gave Tony a belligerent look. "You don't owe me anything."

Tony ignored him and turned back to Kendra.

"I've been wondering when you were going to show up," she said in a mild voice.

"So you just been what, waiting on me to find you?"

"I'd have been happy if I never had to see your face again. I hate you, in case you haven't figured that out yet. If I could have found a way, I would have gone back and killed you for killing my baby."

Tony smiled, appreciating this feistiness in her. He turned to his bodyguards. "This is why I love my Angel so much. 'Cause she's a scrapper, spirited as hell. Makes me work for what I get from her."

"Is that what you call work, beating her half to death, you sick prick?" Garth snarled at him.

Tony's eyes darted to the man beside Garth, who backhanded him, causing his ears to ring. "Shut your mouth," he told Garth.

"I said, don't hurt him!" Kendra yelled. She brought the gun to aim at the man, and as soon as he stepped clear of Garth, she pulled the trigger. The bullet hit him high in the shoulder and the man grunted in surprised pain.

Garth studied her, wondering if this were on purpose or if she had aimed too low. Kendra glanced at him, then back toward the man, tracking him with her gun.

"She shot me!" the man was screaming, clutching his shoulder, blood spurting between his splayed fingers.

"You so much as look at him, I'll kill you," she said, and Garth realized she had only meant to hurt him.

"You bitch," the man muttered and started toward Kendra. A shot rang out and he dropped to his knees with a puzzled look on his face and a neat, round hole in his forehead. He fell face forward into the dirt.

Tony now held a smoking gun in his hand.

Garth wondered briefly where he had gotten it.

"Nobody calls my Angel names," Tony said in a benign way. He turned toward Kendra. "You've been busy."

She forced herself to ignore the dead man. "I knew you would find me. I knew it was only a matter of time."

"So, what, you were getting ready for me?" he asked with amusement.

"I knew you'd show up here one day. I knew you wouldn't just forget me."

Tony studied her for a moment. "You're gonna come back with me," he stated flatly, making this a command.

"Only if you don't kill Garth."

Tony turned and stared at Garth. "What's this? You in love with the guy or something?" He scowled at her.

Kendra remained silent, watching Mark, who now stood beside Garth.

Tony nodded to Mark and he stepped away from Garth and lowered his gun.

Garth started to move toward Kendra and Mark immediately put the gun to his head.

"You kill him, I'm leaving you forever," Kendra said, her voice pressured. Her finger straightened, then curled tighter around the trigger, applying pressure to the gun against her own temple.

Tony glanced at Mark.

Kendra raised her voice. "Your word, Tony. Give me your word you won't kill him. I know you don't break your word, ever."

Tony looked at her with disbelief, then turned and regarded Garth a moment. He glanced back at Kendra and nodded. "Okay, my word. He won't kill him."

"No one will kill him," she clarified.

Tony smiled to show he appreciated this. "No one will kill him, Angel. I give you my word of honor."

"Or hurt him," she insisted.

A look of anger crossed Tony's face. "No one will hurt him. No one will harm a hair on his frigging head, Angel. Now put the gun down and quit playing games."

Tony turned to Mark. "Tie him up."

Mark jerked Garth by the arm to a nearby tree and held him there while Jamille walked over to the horse, pulled out a knife, and cut a length of leather off the bridle. He approached Garth, pulled his hands behind the tree, and tightly bound them.

Garth kept his eyes on Kendra.

"Put down the gun, Angel," Tony commanded irritably when he noticed she had not done as he had requested.

She gave him a maniacal grin. "But I didn't give you my word, Tony."

Tony said, his voice deadly calm, "You kill yourself, I kill him."

Kendra's face changed and she looked with longing toward Garth.

"Run, Keni!" Garth yelled at her. "Get away from here!"

"Yeah, why don't you run," Tony taunted her. "I got two bodyguards here who won't hesitate a minute to take him out, you so much as move. You know that, Angel."

Kendra pulled the gun away from her head and threw it on the ground.

"Now, you gonna come with me or am I gonna have to force you?" Tony asked her.

She stayed where she was, staring at him.

"You know I can't let this go, Angel, you running off like you did. You know you're gonna have to pay for what you did," Tony said, his voice placid.

Kendra seemed to slump in defeat. "I've known that since I left." Her voice sounded dead.

"Let's go," Tony instructed them after ordering Mark to collect Garth's gun as well as the one from the bodyguard lying on the ground.

Kendra ran to Garth, put her arms around him, and hugged him.

Jamille was immediately there, pulling her away.

Garth felt her push something cold and metallic in his hand, knew in an instant the gift she had given him. He looked questioningly into her eyes, showing her his fear for her.

"He won't kill me," she whispered, struggling with the bodyguard, looking Garth in the face. "He has to make me pay first for what I did."

"Get her away from him," Tony said, his expression angry.

"Thank you for saving my life, Garth," Kendra said. There were tears in her eyes. "Thank you for saving my soul," she added, as Jamille pulled her away and forced her to go with them.

"Kendra!" Garth yelled at her.

She turned to look at him over her shoulder.

"Remember!" His eyes darted towards the woods, then back to her.

She nodded, then was gone.

CHAPTER 37

▼

Vincent had traveled off the graveled lane into the woods in order not to be seen but had stayed close enough to keep the road in sight as he maneuvered the slippery forest floor. He glanced up when he heard a gunshot followed by an animal squealing in pain, tripped over an exposed tree root, and fell into a deep ravine. He picked himself up, cursing, and grew frustrated when he didn't feel the familiar bulge beneath his left arm.

Vincent was walking around, stooped over, searching the forest floor, when he heard another shot. He straightened up and turned in a circle, trying to gauge from which direction it had come, but the echo off the mountain ranges seemed to bounce from every direction, so Vincent gave up. He turned his attention back to the forest floor, saw a silver shimmer amongst all the darkened branches and leaves, and trudged in that direction.

His head came up sharply at another retort of a gun. Vincent didn't allow himself the luxury of time to try to ascertain the direction of the shots, instead hurried to his weapon. There was a large stick beside it, almost covering it.

As he reached for the gun, another shot echoed off the mountain peaks. Hesitating, Vincent glanced up the ravine, fighting the feeling of panic threatening to overtake him. When he turned back to the firearm, the stick had moved and was now rising into the air just feet from his legs. A forked tongue slithered toward him, a hissing sound issued from the waving stick.

CHAPTER 38

▼

As soon as they were out of sight, Garth released the button on the switchblade and began sawing at the leather. He had just cut himself free when he caught movement at the edge of the clearing. He glanced up, noting this was one of Tony's thugs, realizing without any surprise at all that Tony was not a man of his word, as he claimed to be.

Garth kept his hands behind the tree as he watched the bodyguard advance toward him.

The man reached him and, without saying a word, pulled out his gun, then a cylindrical object which he began screwing onto the tip of the gun, all the while watching Garth warily.

Garth studied the man, taking note of his nervous demeanor, obvious in the sweat beaded on his forehead and the problem he seemed to be having holding the gun steady while he attached the silencer.

"That so Keni won't hear?" The even tone of Garth's voice caused the man to give him a puzzled glance.

"I was told not to draw any uninvited attention."

"What's your name?"

The bodyguard looked befuddled.

"I'd like to know the name of the man who intends to kill me," Garth said, in a calm voice.

The man nodded grimly. "It's Mark. My name's Mark."

"Where's the car?"

Mark gave him a look of bemused surprise. "You're gonna be dead in thirty seconds, what do you care?"

"'Cause I don't intend to be dead."

"Yeah, well, buddy, if I don't kill you, I'll be dead, so I got no choice. Nothing personal."

Garth brought his arms around with the knife in his left hand and slashed Mark deeply across the right arm, causing him to drop the gun.

"Hey!" Mark yelled, startled.

Garth kicked the gun out of reach while simultaneously slashing with the knife, this time catching the bodyguard in the chest.

Mark grunted loudly and clutched his chest with his left hand.

Garth kicked out, knocking him backwards. Before Mark could recover enough to get up, Garth was straddling him, the knife at his throat.

"Now, I'm only gonna ask this one more time," he said, his eyes deadly. "Where's the car?"

"I don't know, man. I'm lost in these woods," Mark said in a whiny voice.

Garth moved the knife to his face and sliced skin from his temple down to his neck, then brought the knife back to the jugular.

Mark grunted in pain and began squirming beneath Garth, who backhanded him with his left hand, bringing silence. Mark tried bucking Garth off, but he shifted his weight, planted his knee in Mark's groin area, and ground down. Mark screamed in agony.

Garth waited him out.

Mark finally grew silent, cursing Garth with his eyes.

They stared at one another.

Garth didn't say a word as he waited, eyebrows raised.

Mark lay beneath him, panting wildly, his eyes darting left and right, blood running down the side of his face and onto his neck. He was terrified, knowing his life was in danger, but at this point more fearful of what Tony would do to him if he found out he had given information to this man.

"Okay," Garth grunted and put the knife to his other cheek. He ran it down to his throat, leaving a long, red slash.

Mark made gasping, hissing noises.

"Hurts, huh?" Garth put the knife to his forehead.

"Okay, okay," Mark said, the words exploding from him, thinking if he got out of this alive, he'd have to leave the area, go somewhere Tony could never find him.

"I'm waiting." Garth left the knife where he had placed it.

"It's at the bottom of the ridge, at the gate. Tony had Vinnie drive off the road as far as he could."

"Which side?"

"The right."

"Facing toward the gate or away?"

"Toward. There's a little clearing there he drove into, then went further into the woods."

Garth knew where he was talking about. "He leave anybody with the car?"

Mark squinted his eyes against the blood trailing into them and, when Garth nudged him with the knife, nodded. "Yeah, Vinnie, Tony's driver, and the tracker he used to find Angel. They stayed with the car."

Garth thought for a moment. "Okay, I'm gonna get up now. After I'm standing, you stand up, slow, you hear? Then walk over to that tree, lean into it, and put your arms around it. You got that?"

"Yeah, man. Just don't cut me no more," Mark said, sounding like a kid.

Garth eased off him to the right and stood up. He motioned with the knife in his hand for Mark to rise.

Mark sat up, looking pasty, and wiped blood off his face. "I think you've hit a major vein or something. I'm all dizzy."

"You're just scared," Garth said, waiting. "Got all that adrenaline flowing, nothing to do with it."

It seemed to take forever for Mark to get himself righted, then to rise. He stood, wavering.

Garth was growing impatient. "Go to the tree."

"I don't know if I can make it, man. I feel lightheaded," Mark complained.

Garth watched him warily. "You got ten seconds, then I'll just put you out of your misery."

The bodyguard tottered to the tree, leaned against it, and placed his arms around it so that he looked like he was hugging the trunk.

Garth stuck the knife into the bark on the side away from the man, picked up the gun, and tucked it into his waistband. He then retrieved the leather halter, grabbed Mark's hands, and began binding them.

"You ain't gonna leave me here, are you?" Mark asked, his tone anxious.

Garth gave him a look. "You are, I believe, what Keni would call a weenie," he observed drily, tying his hands tighter than needed.

"There's bears out here, all sorts of wild animals." Mark glanced around apprehensively. "I ain't used to being in the mountains. What about snakes? I know there's snakes. I'm scared of snakes."

Garth finished knotting the leather, then stepped back and studied the man. "If I were you, I'd be more afraid of Salvatori coming back and finding me than any animal or snake out here."

"He'll kill me if he finds me like this," Mark said in a resigned manner. "I'd be better off if some bear did get me."

"Then you better pray I kill him first." Garth tucked the knife into his waistband and ran into the forest.

CHAPTER 39

▼

They hadn't traveled very far when Kendra noticed one of Tony's thugs wasn't with them any longer.

She stopped and faced her husband. "Where's Mark?"

Tony shrugged his shoulders, took her elbow, and urged her forward.

Kendra jerked her arm away, turned to him, and drew her face close to his. "If he went back there to Garth, Tony, if you went back on your word, I'll kill you," she said, her voice low, her eyes gleaming.

He laughed, then backhanded her, knocking her on her butt. He watched her with amusement. "Angel, baby, you ain't gonna do anything to me I don't want you to."

Kendra touched the blood trickling from her lip, feeling nothing but hate for this man. Her body jerked when she heard a man cry out in pain.

Tony glanced back toward the clearing.

Kendra gathered dirt and leaves in her hands, stood, and when Tony looked back at her, threw them in his face, blinding him.

Tony cried out as he staggered back, wiping at his eyes.

Kendra managed to kick him in the stomach as hard as she could before the other thug got to her and pulled her away.

Tony bent over, breathing heavily.

Kendra, dangling in Jamille's arms, gave a derisive laugh. "Why, Tony, you're only human after all," she said as if in wonder. "You're not the demon I perceived you to be."

Tony grabbed her out of the man's arms and pulled his fist back to strike her.

"Yeah, go on, hit me," she taunted. "Hitting a woman's easy, isn't it Tony? Someone you outweigh by, what, at least a hundred pounds? So, go on, Tony, hit me, why don't you? Give me more ammunition, more to hate you for."

"Shut the hell up," he said, slapping her instead, causing her ears to ring.

Kendra put her hand to her burning cheek, angry at the tears of pain in her eyes. "If he's dead, I will kill you, Tony. It may not be today, but I give you my word, and unlike you, my word is good, that I will kill you."

Tony glanced at the guard. "Shut her up."

Kendra felt a blow on the back of her neck and sank down into blackness, bleakness.

CHAPTER 40

▼

Garth knew he didn't have time to track them, they had gotten too big a head start on him. Hell, they could be at the car by now. He prayed they wouldn't be.

He rushed down the mountain, taking a shortcut only he and Kendra knew, hoping he would reach the car first. When he got there, he crouched behind a wide tree to study the area, looking for signs of life.

After a few minutes, he cautiously crept forward to inspect the vehicle and the area around it. Crouched over, he crab-walked to the back of the SUV, put his back against it and rocked with his body, making sure someone wasn't hiding inside, ready to jump out at him. The lighter weight of the vehicle, plus the fact that no head popped up or door opened, told him what he wanted to know. He got up, kicking shrubbery aside, and scanned the area around the car. Ascertaining no one was in the vicinity, he backed off a distance, pulled the gun with the silencer from the back of his jeans, and shot the right front tire. He walked to the rear, shot that tire, then to the other side of the car and repeated the procedure. He nodded with satisfaction at the multiple hisses of air escaping from all four tires, rendering it immobile.

He approached the SUV and peered inside, then opened the door and pulled out a cellular phone. He removed the battery from the back, replaced the phone in the car, and tucked the battery pack into his jeans pockets, intending to get rid of it once he was in the woods again.

Back among the trees, he found a hollowed-out log lying on the forest floor, reached in, and placed the battery from the cellular phone well out of sight.

Garth debated on whether to try to find them or lie in wait here at the car. He decided the surest way would be to wait for them, so retreated to a copse of young trees and bushes and squatted down, becoming invisible.

After a minute, Garth knew this wouldn't work for him. He was too restless, too concerned for Kendra's safety, knowing how volatile her husband could be. He decided to go back into the woods, yet stay close enough to the car that he could hear them if they got near it. He left to search for his beloved.

CHAPTER 41

▼

Kendra regained consciousness while being toted by Jamille, Tony's remaining bodyguard. She could taste blood in her mouth, her head felt like it was going to explode, and her stomach rolled violently. She tried raising up. The man stopped.

"Let me down. I'm going to be sick," she said in a raw voice.

Jamille placed Kendra on the ground, and she fell to her knees, heaving. She heard Tony cursing under his breath. Even though she was hurting and miserable, this gave her an instant moment of happiness; she knew he couldn't stand to hear anyone regurgitate.

After she was finished, Kendra walked away from the vomitus and sat down heavily. Feeling dizzy, she put her head in her hands.

"Let's go," Tony commanded, walking toward her.

"Give me a minute. I think I'm going to be sick again." Kendra was glad inside when Tony retreated away from her.

She sat, bent over at the waist, her head in her hands, willing her body to function and her head to clear, trying to gather her strength.

Tony and the guard stood away from her, talking in low voices.

Kendra surreptitiously glanced around her, gauging whether she could get away from them. She recognized this part of the forest. They were close to the bottom of the mountain, where she was sure they had parked the car. In order to buy more time, she turned her back on Tony and his thug and made gagging noises, pretending to throw up once more, while studying the forest floor. It would be an uphill climb. Her head hurt and she felt dizzy; she wondered if he had hit her hard enough to cause a concussion. The fact that she had passed out weighed heavily on her mind. Would she be able to outrun them? she wondered.

The advantage to her was that she was familiar with this area and they weren't. However, she knew Tony's thugs stayed in tiptop shape: one of Tony's rules. If she ran and they caught her, she didn't want to think about it. Kendra sat back down and rested her head on her knees, cursing Tony, hating him. Please, God, she prayed silently, let Garth be alive. Please, let him have gotten away. Please, if one of us has to die to pay for our happiness, let it be me. She had to bite her tongue to keep the tears from exploding out of her and rubbed her hands violently against her eyes.

She heard movement to her side and glanced that way. Garth was hunkered down low, staring intently at her. She felt her facial muscles bunching together, forming a smile, then remembered where she was and who was near. She placed her hand over her heart, signaling her love to him, letting him know she was aware he was there, her heart soaring at the sight of him. She glanced back toward Tony and his bodyguard.

Kendra realized she needed to distract Tony. She looked back at Garth, fearful for his safety.

Garth put a finger to his lips in a shushing gesture, then held up the knife and made a throwing motion toward her.

She barely nodded before bending over and making gagging noises in order to cover up the sound of the knife landing beside her.

Kendra glanced at Tony and the bodyguard, who were ignoring her. She bent down and retrieved the knife, placed the shaft inside her palm, then stood and walked toward them. She had to force herself not to look at Garth.

Kendra deliberately made her gait unsteady and tried to appear in worse shape than she actually was.

Tony turned to look at her. "You ready?"

Kendra didn't answer as she moved toward them.

Tony gave her a worried look. "You feel like you can walk or you want to be carried?"

"I think he really hurt me, Tony," Kendra said, making her voice weak, playing on his sympathy. "My head feels like it's gonna explode, I'm sick at my stomach, I'm dizzy. I don't know if I can walk."

"Why'd you have to hit her so hard for?" Tony angrily asked Jamille.

"You told me to shut her up," Jamille said in a defensive manner.

"I didn't mean to hurt her!"

"But I didn't. I only tapped her."

"When we get back, I'm gonna have a doctor check her out, and she better be okay, or you're gonna be hurting," Tony threatened.

Garth, working his way toward them as quietly as he could, listening to this exchange, thought, What a sick prick.

Kendra put her hand on the back of her neck and rolled her head as if it were hurting her greatly. She glanced around for Garth who was behind Tony and to the side now. She surreptitiously winked, as if she had heard his thoughts.

That wink gave Garth pause. Is she having fun with this? he wondered to himself. He immediately dismissed the thought.

Kendra walked unsteadily toward her husband and stopped a few feet away.

Tony now looked at her with concern. "Angel, baby, I didn't mean for him to hurt you. You know I wouldn't stand for that."

Kendra had to bite her tongue to keep from responding, thinking he couldn't stand for anyone else to hurt her, but it sure didn't bother him to do the deed himself. She stood, swaying slightly, now wiping at her eyes, as if the pain were causing tears.

"Carry her," Tony commanded his man.

Jamille started toward her, frowning widely.

Kendra waited until he was right at her, ready to pick her up.

Jamille registered the click of the blade being shot at the same time he felt it pierce his side. His eyes widened with alarm, then pain. He stepped back from Kendra, clutching his side, blood running between his fingers. He looked at her with disbelief and made a low, grunting noise.

Tony, standing behind him, not knowing what had transpired, looked with askance at Jamille as he moved away from his wife. "I said carry her, you dumb shit." He moved toward the man in order to cuff him, show him who was boss, but was thrown forward when Garth landed on his back, pushing him down. Tony responded quickly, twisting around and swinging at Garth with his right fist.

Garth dodged the first blow, but the one coming from the left caught him by surprise and stunned him for a moment.

Kendra didn't want to kill Jamille but didn't like the look in his eyes when he turned from her and moved toward Garth. She knew she had to divert his attention away from aiding Tony and back to her. She swiped at his thigh with the knife, trying to get to the hamstring, trying to cripple him.

Jamille roared like a bull when he felt the knife penetrate. He brought his arm around and cuffed Kendra with the back of his hand, knocking her off balance. The knife flew out of her hand when she landed on her rear.

Tony surprised Garth, scrabbling forward, carrying Garth on his back. He reached out, then quickly twisted around. Garth felt a stinging sensation in his left shoulder, looked down, and saw Tony had somehow managed to plant the knife there.

Using his right fist, Garth knocked Tony's hand away from him, and the knife went flying away. Tony twisted once again, almost threw Garth off, and went after the weapon, crawling on his stomach. Garth, riding him like a little kid playing horsey with his dad, pulled his gun and placed it at Tony's temple. This immediately halted his struggles.

Garth looked for Kendra. The bodyguard, after ascertaining the leg wound wasn't serious, was heading her way.

"Hold it right there! Don't go near her!" Garth yelled, pointing the gun at Jamille.

Tony seized the opportunity to try to throw Garth off his back.

Garth took the time to rudely tap the crown of his head with the gun. "Next time, you'll wake up with a headache." Tony went still.

The bodyguard turned, saw Tony on the ground, and charged. Garth brought the gun up and fired at his knee. Jamille collapsed, grabbing his leg, screaming in agony.

Kendra searched frantically for the knife, glancing continually at Garth and the two men on the ground.

"Get him!" Tony yelled at his man when he had quieted. His voice was muffled; Garth's weight was making it hard for him to breathe.

Breathing harshly, Jamille sat up and glared at Garth. Garth pointed the gun at him. "Don't make one move, or the next one will kill you."

Jamille remained still while watching Garth. Garth could practically hear the tumblers in his brain as he assessed this situation and what he could do about it. Garth knew he was having an inner battle about whether to face Garth now or face Tony later if he didn't do anything.

Apparently deciding Tony was the more dangerous choice, Jamille rose quickly, but before he could stand completely, immediately went down on his knees, stared blankly at Garth for a second, then fell forward.

Kendra was behind him, holding a thick branch. "Strike one!" she said, almost happily.

Garth glanced at her again, wondering, then placed the gun back against Tony's temple. "I'm going to get off you. Wait till I'm standing, then get on your knees."

Now that he had him, Garth wasn't sure what they should do with him. The way Kendra was acting, he didn't know if he wanted to let her loose with this guy.

Garth eased off and rose as he pointed the gun at Tony's prostrate form. "Okay, up." He tracked Tony's movements with the firearm.

"You're gonna die for this," Tony said in a low voice.

"What, for messing with the big guy?" Kendra taunted him as she stood beside Garth.

"And you are going to pay, Angel. This won't go unpunished," Tony snarled at her.

"I'm so scared," Kendra said, sounding anything but.

Garth glanced at her, and when he turned back to Tony, was staring at a chrome hole aimed right at him. He heard Kendra gasp.

Kendra threw the branch at Tony and it landed on his arm at the same moment he pulled the trigger.

Garth felt a tearing sensation in his leg and immediately collapsed.

"You shit!" Kendra screamed at Tony, who was now holding his arm with the gun dangling limply from his hand. She kicked him in the chest and sent him sprawling. She followed his hand, the one still holding the gun, and kicked it.

Tony roared as the gun skittered across the forest floor and scrambled after it.

Kendra retrieved the log and struck him on the back of the head. Tony went limp, sprawling on his belly.

Kendra recovered the gun and tucked it into her jeans at the waist. She ran over to Garth, a worried expression on her face.

"Let me see, let me see." She pulled his hands away from his leg, where blood was spurting in a steady stream.

"Oh, please, no," she said, as if in prayer. She shucked her belt out of her jeans and used it to make a tourniquet for his leg, wrapping it around his thigh and cinching it tight.

Garth hissed in pain.

"Get up." She placed her shoulder under his to help him. His leg wouldn't cooperate and Garth lost his balance and would have fallen if she hadn't kept him anchored.

"Stay up, damnit," she said, her voice hard, almost shrill. She glanced at Tony, who hadn't moved.

Garth tried again and managed to stay upright this time, swaying slightly.

"Move," Kendra barked at him, urging him forward, afraid for Garth. She took one last quick look at Tony and was relieved to see he was still down.

CHAPTER 42

▼

Vincent froze for a moment as he watched the snake rear its triangular head, then hurled himself backwards. The snake struck at the space formerly occupied by his torso. "Shit!" he yelled, landing on his side. The serpent rose into the air once more, hissing, its tongue slithering obscenely from its mouth. Vincent briefly debated whether he should freeze or move, and the movie *Jurassic Park* came to mind. What was it with reptiles? They sensed movement? Heat? If you were perfectly still, could they even see you? He forced himself to breathe shallowly through his nose, forced himself to remain still, watching the weaving snake.

A shot rang out, bouncing off the rocky walls of the summit. Vincent visibly startled and became alarmed when the snake turned its ugly head his way. But the serpent was either bothered by the sound waves from the shot or simply wasn't interested in him anymore. It lowered its body to the forest floor and slithered away.

Vincent quickly rose, retrieved the gun, snugged it into his shoulder holster, made sure to secure it, then began to climb. He managed to scale his way out of the ravine but had somehow gone far astray from the road and wondered if he had climbed out the wrong side. He turned around in circles, cursing his stupidity. He fought the urge to panic as he pushed himself to find the location from which the shots were being fired.

CHAPTER 43

▼

Somehow they made it to a nearby cave they had set up as a safe place. Kendra bore Garth's weight against her and continuously urged him to keep moving, to get away with her to safety. She constantly cast her eyes behind them in search of their adversary.

Once ensconced within the cave, she helped Garth lay down on the dirt floor, then retrieved the lantern they had previously placed on a ledge within the rock wall. She reached into her jeans, pulled out a butane lighter and lit the lantern, even though it was still daylight outside and there was light filtering into the cave.

Kendra returned to Garth, held the lantern close to his shoulder and studied it, then moved to his leg.

Garth felt woozy, a great need to go to sleep.

"Stay awake, Garth!" She shook his injured shoulder, causing him to yell out with pain.

She undid her belt and rewound it around his upper thigh, cinching it as tight as she could, trying to stop the steady flow of blood.

Searing pain traveled up Garth's leg into his chest. "Shit!" he snarled.

"Ain't that the truth," Kendra panted.

She hurried to their hidey-hole, took out the knife they had hidden there, and returned. She released the blade and cut open his shirt to reveal the wound in his shoulder. She gingerly turned him on his side, cut the shirt around to the back, and prodded with her fingers.

Garth grit his teeth.

Kendra helped him lie back. "Knife went straight in. It's not bleeding much, so I don't think he hit a major vein."

She returned to the hidey-hole, retrieved a first-aid kid she had hidden there, knelt beside Garth, and rummaged through it. She pulled out Betadine and a small tube, threw them on the ground beside him, then took off her shirt and began to tear it into strips.

Garth watched all of this in a haze, tracking but not understanding what she was doing.

When Kendra had finished with the shirt, she leaned down close his face. "This is gonna hurt, sweetie, but I have to do it."

He nodded.

She picked up one of the strips and tenderly wiped around the wound in his shoulder. She threw it down, picked up the Betadine and squirted it directly into the wound, then dried the area as much as she could.

Garth grunted in pain and sweat broke out on his face. Kendra put down the Betadine, picked up the tube, took the top off, and held it up for him to see. "Crazy Glue."

"Wha?"

"They use it in hospitals instead of stitches. Learned that the hard way. Let's see if it'll plug this gash up."

"Damn, Kendra, you're liable to poison my system you put that crap in a knife wound," he said weakly.

"I don't guess it's gonna hurt you too much." She bent toward his shoulder and pulled the shirt open, exposing the wound. She gave him an impish grin. "'Course, when they try to get the bandage off, that might hurt a bit, seeing as how it's gonna be stuck to the glue which will be stuck to your beautiful skin."

"You punishing me for something I don't remember doing?" Garth asked her, trying for levity.

Ignoring this, she squeezed contents from the tube onto his shoulder and held the flayed flesh together, letting the glue bond. After a minute, she let go and waited to see if it held. Grunting with satisfaction, she drew one of the strips toward her, folded it in half, then again. She placed the bandage over the wound, took two more strips, tied them together, and proceeded to wrap them around his shoulder, securing the bandage.

Garth kept his teeth gritted together, sporadically expelling breathing sounds of agony as she maneuvered his shoulder, which Kendra ignored.

"Darlin', you think that was bad, wait till I get to your leg," she murmured, tying her dressing.

Garth lay back, sweat running down his face. "Why don't you just go ahead and kill me?" he grunted.

Kendra brought her face close to his and waited until he looked her in the eyes. "You go and die on me, Garth Fisher, I swear to God, I will hunt you down wherever you may go in your next life and make you as miserable as hell."

He laughed weakly. "I think you probably would."

She moved to his leg and checked her tourniquet, then gently probed around, running her hand under his leg, feeling. "Bullet must have gone clean through. I can't feel it in there anywhere, and the bleeding's slowed some." She used the knife to cut the jeans away from the bloodied area and held the lantern close, studying his leg more closely. "Looks like it dug a furrow out of your thigh. It didn't get close enough to nick any bone that I can see." She picked up the Betadine and squirted it directly into the deep gash, then began dabbing at the lengthy wound with a strip of cloth.

Garth, who had begun to drift, screamed.

"Thought that'd get your attention," she said mildly, picking up the glue.

"Oh, damn," he murmured, watching her.

"You're got a good-sized laceration here, darlin'. I don't know if this will work, but I think I can at least get most of the bleeding to stop." Kendra looked at him. "It's gonna hurt a hell of a lot, Garth. You might want to bite down on something."

"I'll manage," he grunted, laying his head back.

"Mr. macho man to the extreme," she said, almost distractedly, then placed her hands on each side of the wound and tried to squeeze it together.

"Aaaaahhhhh!" Garth yelled.

Kendra picked up the Crazy Glue and seemed to pour most of the contents over the jagged tear, all the while squeezing the skin together.

It was all Garth could do to keep from writhing in agony. He started seeing black spots in front of his eyes and knew he would pass out if she didn't stop.

She finally released the skin, undid the belt, and sat waiting. "Still seeping." She grabbed the tube again.

"Keni, let it go," he muttered.

"Hell no," she answered, going back to work.

After Kendra had emptied the contents of the tube onto the ragged wound, she tied more strips together and tightly wound them around Garth's leg.

"You cut off the circulation, I'm liable to lose that leg," he said, his voice shaking.

"Baby, I'd rather have you without one leg than not at all."

After she had tied the bandage, Kendra sat on her knees, lantern held high, watching for seepage. "Bleeding's slowed way down," she finally said.

Rising, she took another strip and tied it around her forehead.

Garth noticed she had somehow sustained a cut on her scalp, from which blood was trickling, gathering at the band above her eyes. "You okay?" he asked, concerned for her.

Kendra nodded, took the band out of her ponytail, and put it in her mouth. She raked her hair back with her fingers, then resecured it.

Garth raised up on his elbows and stared at Kendra with her flannel headband, her dark hair pulled into a ponytail, wearing a white tank top, no bra, her breasts molded against the material, jeans highlighting her long legs, her hiking boots adding height. He imagined if he could see her aura now, it would be dark blue spiked with bright, neon pink. "Jesus, Keni, you're the most beautiful thing I've ever seen," he said weakly.

She detected admiration in his voice and smiled.

"You remind me of a warrior princess going off to do battle," he finished, laying back.

"In a way, I am." She returned to their hidey-hole and retrieved the .38 semi-automatic they had left there.

Garth sat up straight, alarmed. "No!"

Kendra ignored him. She checked the gun for ammunition, reached into the hole, and drew out more.

"Kendra, damnit, listen to me," Garth said in a panicked voice.

She turned to him. "Garth, I have to get to him before he gets to his car." She tucked the ammo into her pockets and the gun into the waistband at her back, much the same way he had done. "He'll call for help if he gets down the mountain, you know that, and this place will be covered with his people. We can't let that happen. I should have killed him back there, but I didn't want to take the time."

"It's okay," he said with relief. "I've already disabled the car, pulled the battery out of the cell phone, hid it."

"He always keeps an extra phone in the glove compartment. Did you find that one?"

"No," Garth said, disappointed.

"It's okay. You had no way of knowing about it."

"There's two more out there, Keni. Stay here, baby. Let me go."

Kendra glanced at the entrance to the cave, then returned her attention to him. "Two more? How do you know this?"

Garth struggled to sit up. "That bodyguard Tony sent back for me, he said Tony left Vinnie and the tracker they used to find you at the car, but when I got there, they were gone. They're in these woods somewhere."

Kendra thought for a moment. "Vincent helped me escape, so chances are he'll help me now," she said as if speaking to herself.

Garth struggled to rise. "I'll go."

Kendra gently pushed him back down. "You're too weak. You've lost too much blood." She knelt beside him, picked up the knife, and retracted the blade. Garth watched as she placed the handle against her wrist, picked up another swatch of cloth, and bound the knife to the inside of her arm. "Besides, this is my battle, not yours," she said, concentrating on what she was doing. "This has been coming for a long time now. I'm at least owed this, don't you think?"

"He'll kill you," Garth said in a raspy voice.

"He's like a cat with a mouse." Kendra returned to the hidey-hole and pulled out a canteen. She knelt beside Garth once more, unscrewed the cap, poured some water on another strip, and wiped his face with it.

"He'll want to play with me first, torture me, if you will, for what I've done, for not coming to heel." She looked at him and Garth was shocked to see she was smiling.

"But I am no longer the mouse in this game, thanks to you." She took a swig from the canteen, wiped her mouth with the back of her hand, then put the canteen to his lips, tilted it, and filled his mouth with water before he could respond.

After Garth had taken a drink, Kendra replaced the cap and put the canteen beside him. She stood up, walked to the mouth of the cave, and turned back to him. "I don't have much time and I've got to reach him before he gets help. If I'm not back in an hour, get out of here, okay? I don't want them to find you."

Garth was ashamed to find his eyes filled with tears. "I can't bear the thought of losing you, Keni. I don't think I can live with that," he said in an anguished voice.

Giving him an angelic smile, Kendra came to him, went down on both knees beside him, and took his face in her hands. "Oh, love," she said tenderly. "Whether in this life or the next, we will be together, Garth. We're meant to be." She kissed his lips quickly and was gone before he could reply.

CHAPTER 44

▼

Kendra found Tony where she had left him, sitting on an outcropping of rocks this time, holding a handkerchief to the back of his head.

He looked up when he heard her, studied her a minute, then said idly, as if nothing at all had happened between them, "I was just debating whether to go find you or go find the car."

"You shouldn't have bothered worrying about me," she replied, guardedly watching him.

He smirked at her. "Yeah, and why's that?"

"'Cause I'm not going back with you," she answered, keeping her distance.

He glared at her. "That point is not negotiable, Angel," he said in a hard voice.

She bared her teeth at him, reached behind her, drew the gun out of her waist-band, and cocked it. She was glad to see his eyes flicker.

Kendra approached the prone guard, who was lying in the same position he had been when they left. She nudged him with her foot while keeping the gun aimed at Tony.

"He's dead," Tony said.

She looked at him.

"I won't have anyone in my camp that has to sit and debate whether they're gonna help me," he said in an impassive voice.

She looked closer at the guard and could see his neck was broken.

"So you just killed him."

Tony barely glanced at the guy. "He knew the rules."

Kendra decided to ignore the dead man. She was agitated by the fact that she couldn't pull the trigger and kill her husband. She had hoped it would be that easy but knew in the deep recesses of her mind that he would have to provoke his death. This made her uneasy.

Kendra tried to quell her shaking body, tried to keep the gun steady. She knew she couldn't reason with him but felt she had to try. "You got two choices, Tony. You can either go back down the mountain, get in your car, leave, forget about me, or you can stay here. But by the time this is over, one of us will be on this mountain forever, if you get my drift."

Tony gave her an irritated look. "I'm not leaving without you, Angel."

"If you're worried about me testifying against you, forget about it. I'm not that stupid. All I'm asking from you is that you go, get out of my life, and let me live mine the way I want to, away from you, without fear of you."

"Damn, Angel, you look like shit," Tony said, as if he hadn't even heard her, running his eyes over her body.

"As if I care what you think."

"You're lost weight, babe. I'm gonna have to fatten you up when I get you home."

"The getting me home point is not negotiable," she mimicked him.

Tony glanced behind her. "Where's your boyfriend?"

"Out of the picture, thanks to you," she answered, hoping this was a lie.

"But you still want to stay," he said, indicating he didn't believe her.

"I just want away from you." Kendra heard a twig snap and glanced around.

Ignoring this, Tony rose to his feet, directing her attention back to him. "Away from me?" he asked incredulously. "Shit, Angel, I've only given the world to you. You have everything you could ever want. You don't even have to ask for anything, it's all there at your beck and call, and still you're not happy."

She gritted her teeth. "The only time I have ever been happy in my life has been since I left you. I have found that there's a lot to be said for freedom."

"Freedom? You had all the freedom in the world when you were with me."

"Oh yeah? Well, what about all those goons you had trailing me everywhere I went?"

"That was for your own protection, and you probably didn't even appreciate that," he said snidely.

"I don't love you, Tony," Kendra said, her voice low. "Let me go. That's all I'm asking from you."

"I will not let you go!" he roared.

She startled and the gun waved wildly until she got it under control.

Tony pointed his finger at her. "You did once upon a time love me, Angel, whether you will admit it or not, and you will again."

"The only time I ever cared about you was when I was too young to see you for the cruel, vindictive man you are," she shouted at him. Her finger bore down on the trigger and she realized she was very close to killing him then.

Tony scowled at her, then glanced behind her.

Kendra angled around so she could see what he was looking at. She didn't discern anything, so turned back to Tony, whose attention was now on her.

"I was never cruel nor vindictive with you," he said, his voice low.

"You killed my mother and my father!" she screamed at him. "You made me watch while you beat Tommy to death, you sick bastard. How much more cruel can you get?" Kendra wiped at the tears rolling down her face: tears of frustration, tears of anger. Her inner voice kept urging her to just pull the damn trigger, but she couldn't do it. She knew she wouldn't be able to live with herself, killing someone in cold blood. Even if it was Tony.

He gave her a look of concern. "Angel, baby, when will you understand, I didn't kill your mother. Your old man did that. The only part I played was helping him get rid of her body 'cause he threatened to turn me into the DEA if I didn't. I swear, baby, that was it." He tried giving her an innocent look.

"I don't believe you." Kendra swiped at her eyes with her left hand and the gun wavered slightly in her right.

"As for your father, hell, anything could have happened to him. And why should you care anyway? He didn't love you. All he used you for was a punching bag. I took you away from that, you know." Now Tony was trying to sound benevolent.

"Yeah and turned me into your own," she spat.

"You only got what you deserved."

"You made me watch you kill Tommy." Her voice was low, tortured. "I will never forgive you for that."

Tony held his hands up, palms out. "You had to be taught a lesson, babe, you know that. You let him sweet-talk you into leaving with him. I found out he worked for KPD, was gonna use you to testify against me."

"That's your story."

Tony grew angry. "Okay, let's cut the shit. I've explained all I'm going to to you. You've had your temper-tantrum, now it's time to go home and get back to being my wife."

Kendra struggled with herself, trying to gain composure, knowing he could easily overtake her if she lost control. "You had no right to kill my baby," she said, when she could talk. She realized she was trying to provoke him, trying to get him to say the right thing that would trigger enough emotion in her to kill him.

"You gotta look at it from my perspective," he said, his voice gentle, coaxing. "You're my wife, Angel. I can't have you ruining that beautiful body of yours by having babies. You wanted a kid, you should have told me. I could have gotten you one easy."

"That was my baby, in my body!" she yelled, startling him. "You aren't God. You can't decide who or what lives and dies."

"Ah, but baby, I am god in my universe," Tony said in a hard voice. "And you are my wife and you will do as I say, Angel, no doubt about it. You understand me? Now quit playing games with me, put down that friggin gun, and get over here."

She laughed harshly, surprising him. "I don't think so." She brought the gun up and pointed it at him.

Kendra saw Tony's eyes dart to her left before she actually felt the movement, turned, and was caught in a bear hug as a man put his arms around her. He crushed her against him, jerked the gun away from her, and threw it on the ground at their feet.

CHAPTER 45

▼

Garth lay back, trying to fight the feeling of panic that threatened to overtake him. He knew if anything happened to Kendra, he would never forgive himself. He had had his chance to save her and, once again, had failed.

Forget this shit, he thought, sitting up, then standing, almost falling in the process when his leg threatened to buckle. He stood, swaying slightly, feeling lightheaded and nauseous.

"Get moving, damnit," he whispered to himself, forcing his feet forward.

His leg at first wouldn't cooperate with his body, did not want to move in synch, and he had to literally use his hands to guide it, picking it up, moving it ahead, putting it down, dragging it behind him as he moved forward with the other. Eventually, it seemed to loosen up and function as a somewhat rebellious appendage.

Sweat poured from every pore of his body as he forced himself to move. He had bled through the bandage on his shoulder and could feel blood running down his leg, but ignored this, now intent on getting back to where they had left Tony, praying Kendra would still be there.

CHAPTER 46

▼

Kendra struggled with the man, flailing with her penned-down arms, kicking with her legs until she was exhausted, then went limp, resting in his arms.

"About time you got here," Tony said to his driver, after she was quiet.

"I been all over this mountain trying to find you," Vincent said, loosening his grip on Kendra.

She leaned against him and tried to regain her breath, her strength.

Tony tucked the handkerchief in his back pocket and gingerly felt the back of his head. "Think you can find the car?"

"Yeah, I think I remember the way back," Vincent said, distractedly, watching Tony, loosely holding Kendra by his side.

Tony brought his hand around and studied the bloody fingers. "Angel, baby, you are gonna pay for this big time," he said, showing them to her.

"You think so?" she asked, her eyes glistening.

Tony seemed surprised at this response, but recovered quickly, commanding, "Get over here."

"Why don't you make me, Tony." Kendra held her arm flat against her side and flexed her right wrist, pulling at the tip of the knife.

Tony watched her, waiting. "You'll only make it worse on yourself if I do."

Kendra tried to look to him as if she were unsure what to do, while she tugged at the knife. Feeling the strip of cloth around her right wrist loosen, then the handle of the switchblade fall easily into her palm, she caught it and released the blade. She brought her arm around and swiped at Vincent with it, pulling back at the last minute. She heard him yell out and saw blood.

Kendra quickly put the knife in her left hand, swung her leg behind Vincent's ankles and kicked him, toppling him. She dropped to the ground, grabbed the gun, and stood, holding it in front of her, stopping Tony's advance.

"What the hell do you think you're doing?" Tony asked with disbelief.

Kendra glanced at Vincent to make sure he wasn't going to be a problem, then back to her husband, who had murder in his eyes. She cocked the gun. "I've been chasing demons long enough, Tony."

"You want to see a demon, I'll show you a demon," he said menacingly, advancing toward her.

Kendra put her index finger on the trigger and pulled it. Although she aimed for his chest, the bullet went high and struck him in the shoulder.

The impact stopped his progress and sent him stumbling back a couple of steps. Tony got his footing while giving her an incredulous look. His hand went to the wounded area, followed by his eyes, which then came to hers and were the deadliest, coldest eyes she had ever seen in her life. A demon's eyes.

Kendra held the gun with both hands. "Do me one favor, Tony. When you get to hell, give my regards to my father." She pulled the trigger once more.

The bullet caught Tony in the chest, right at the heart, forcing him back. He lost his balance and fell backwards, then lay on the ground, not moving.

Kendra approached Vincent, who was struggling to sit up. Blood was trickling between the fingers clutching his neck. He stared at her.

Kendra gave him a concerned look. "I hope I didn't hit the jugular. I didn't mean to hurt you, Vinnie. I tried to pull the swing short." Of all the men who clustered around Tony, Vincent was the only one who had ever shown any compassion toward her. She had a soft spot for him.

Vincent pulled his fingers away from the wound and studied them. "If you hit the artery, there'd be more blood than this."

Kendra knelt beside him.

"You kill him?"

She glanced at Tony, who hadn't moved. "I think so," she said, then added, "I hope so."

"You better pray you did. I don't think he'll forgive this one, Angel."

She grimaced. "If I put this gun down, are you gonna be nice?"

He gave her a questioning look.

"I need to know you haven't gone back to his side. We should put something on that cut, Vinnie. I don't want you to bleed to death."

He nodded wearily.

Kendra placed the gun beside her foot, took off the strip of cloth she had worn for a headband, and wrapped it around Vincent's neck.

After she was finished, Kendra sat back. "I think I need to get you to a doctor, Vin." She gave him a sorrowful look. "I'm really sorry I cut you like that."

"It looks worse than it is," he said, sounding macho.

They stared at one another.

"I could have stopped him," he said in a low voice, "but he saw me before I could get close enough to take a kill shot. I didn't know if he had a gun on him and didn't want to chance it."

She nodded. "I thought so. I was counting on you not to."

"I thought you might be." He gave her a look. "Hell, Angel, you got to get more practice in. I had to jump up and then back to try to make that kick look better than it was."

She smiled at him. "I kind of figured that. Here, let me help you up."

"Go check Tony first. Let me rest a minute."

"You sure you're okay?" Kendra asked, worried.

"A little, bitty thing like you can't do me much harm."

"I sure hope not." Kendra picked up the gun, stood, and walked toward her demon.

Kendra stood over Tony with the gun pointed at him, watching for signs of life. A thought nudged at her brain. She could see blood around the area of his right shoulder but none on his chest. She wondered if the bullet had gone directly into the heart, causing the heart to stop pumping and the blood to immediately stop flowing. She turned to Vincent. "I shot him in the chest, but I don't see any blood there." Then she remembered something. "Was he wearing a vest?"

Vincent's eyes widened, and simultaneously, Kendra felt her feet being pulled out from underneath her. She landed on her back and the breath exploded out of her. The gun flew from her hand.

Kendra curled up on her side, trying to catch her breath, trying to think, cursing herself for not realizing Tony had the damn vest on, something he wore a lot.

Tony stood over her, shouting angrily.

She closed her eyes and put her hands over her ears, shutting him out.

He reached down, grabbed one arm, pulled her up, and jammed the gun in her face.

Her eyes widened with alarm.

"Don't even think about it," Kendra heard Garth say, his words calm, his voice even.

She burst into tears at the sight of him. Blood seemed to cover him from head to foot. She didn't see how he could be standing, much less have traveled this far.

Garth glanced at Kendra, and the dream eyes and the real ones seemed to merge. He fought the feeling of dread in his body and silently prayed, Please, God, don't let me fail her, please let me protect her, please don't let her die.

"Let her go," he said, and Kendra noticed he had a gun trained on Tony.

Vincent had gone to stand close to Tony and was watching this exchange with a gun in his hand.

"Kill him," Tony said.

Vincent looked at Garth, who didn't even spare him a glance, then back to Tony. "I don't think so."

Tony gave him an incredulous look and, pulling the gun from Kendra, started to turn.

"I think I'll kill you instead." Vincent placed the gun against Tony's temple and pulled the trigger.

Kendra screamed as blood and gore washed over her, kept screaming until Garth took her in his arms.

CHAPTER 47

▼

After Garth and Vincent made sure Tony was dead, they left his body where he had collapsed and the three of them started back to Garth's cabin. Garth walked between Kendra and Vincent, his arms around the shoulders of each, but leaned heavily against Vincent, who bore his weight without complaint.

Once there, Kendra placed an emergency call to Thad to come tend to Garth, who refused to go to a hospital. She checked Vincent's neck wound more closely and was glad to see it was only superficial. After Thad arrived and assured her Garth wasn't going to bleed to death, Kendra left them to shower. She scrubbed fiercely at her skin, trying to get all the blood and gore off, gagging at the stench, crying tears of relief, tears she did not want the men to see.

When she joined them, Thad had finished tending to Garth's leg and was now addressing his shoulder wound, which was barely seeping, listening as Vinnie and Garth told him what had happened.

Thad admired Kendra's work with the Crazy Glue.

She gave Garth a look when he did this.

Garth weakly rolled his eyes.

"You'll pay for that one," she teased him.

While Thad cleaned and applied antiseptic to Vincent's neck wound, Kendra filled Vincent in on what had happened before he came upon the scene.

Kendra and Garth had a long discussion with Vincent about what to do with Tony and the two bodyguards he had killed.

Vincent thought awhile as he idly rubbed at the bandage on his neck. He finally told them he would handle it.

Thad was checking Kendra's head wound, making sure it didn't require stitches. She put her hand over his to stop him and stared at Vincent. "Meaning?"

"You don't want to know."

"I think I have to," she told him, her voice low.

He raised his eyebrows at her.

"I don't want to have to tiptoe around anymore, Vinnie. I have to know I'm safe here, that I can actually have a life for once."

He studied her a long moment. "Okay," he finally said, more to himself than her. He turned to Garth. "There like a cliff or a bluff around here? Something with a long drop?"

Garth and Thad looked at one another.

"I'll show you," Thad said.

"Can I get the car to it?" Vincent asked.

Thad nodded. "There's a service road goes right to it."

Vincent turned back to Kendra. "I'm gonna go get the car, drive it up the mountain, gather up the bodies, put them in it, then send it off the side of the mountain. I'll rig it up so it explodes when it hits and'll burn 'em all beyond recognition."

She thought about this.

"Oh, yeah. I almost forgot, I left one of the bodyguards tied to a tree," Garth said in a weak voice.

"Mark, the one Tony sent after Garth. I forgot about him," Kendra said. She turned to Vincent. "He's in the clearing. I'll take you to him."

"Good, he can help," Vincent said.

"He won't get in your way on this?" she asked with a worried look on her face.

Vincent shook his head. "Hell, Angel, Tony was out of control. We all knew sooner or later, somebody was going to have to do something about him. You can't just go around killing people for no particular reason. He didn't seem to understand that."

"Shoot, Mark was more worried about Tony finding him tied to a tree than me shooting him," Garth said. "I don't think he'll be any kind of a problem."

He lay back, then sat up again. "What about the tracker?"

Vincent shrugged. "He's long gone. Didn't want to be involved with anything that was going down and took off the minute Tony started up the mountain."

Garth nodded. "Oh, about the car, I think you're going to have a problem moving it. I shot all the tires."

Vincent groaned.

"I'll run you to Wal-Mart," Thad said brightly. "They carry just about any size. I can help you change them."

"You're all right." Vincent gave Thad an appreciative look, causing him to beam.

Thad told Kendra he'd lead Vincent to the clearing and help him release Mark before they headed to Wal-Mart.

After they left, Kendra curled up beside Garth on the couch. She wrinkled her nose. "You need a shower."

"I think I'll just rest a minute." Garth could feel her staring at him and glanced at her.

There were tears in her eyes.

He drew back and gave her a questioning look.

"You're my hero," Kendra said, "you know that?"

"Yeah, well, guess what, babe, you're my hero too." He put his hand underneath her chin and kissed her, meaning it. then lay back.

Kendra, thinking he had fallen asleep, started to rise to clean up the mess Thad had made while dressing the two men's wounds.

Garth tugged her back down beside him.

"Are you all right?" she asked, worriedly. "Do you need anything?"

"Just you," he said, giving her an intent look.

She smiled at him.

"There's something I've been meaning to ask you," he said, his voice weak. He was so tired he didn't think he could stay awake for very long, but he had to ask, and he wanted to do it now before he lost his nerve.

She stroked his face with her hand. "What?"

"Will you marry me, Kendra? Will you stay with me on this mountaintop, have a family with me, grow old with me?"

She burst into tears.

He wasn't so sleepy anymore, becoming alarmed at this, cursing himself for being so stupid as to think she would actually want to be his wife.

He grunted when she threw herself into his arms.

"Yes! Oh, yes, Garth, I'll marry you. Oh, I can't tell you how happy you've made me."

He was wide awake now.

CHAPTER 48

▼

Their wedding was held outdoors, on top of the mountain, on a beautiful, clear day in September. Kendra and Garth marveled, as they always did, at the beautiful scenery God had displayed for them as they stood before a preacher. Thad played the dual roles of best man and man of honor. The only other attendees were Vincent and Chloe and the preacher's wife, who had a keyboard with her and solemnly played the wedding march as Kendra walked down a makeshift aisle upon which Chloe had placed daises and wild flowers.

Afterward, Kendra and Garth held a small reception at the cabin, surprised at the number of people who dropped by during the afternoon, wishing them well, welcoming Kendra to their community. They were stunned to learn that the secret they felt they had been keeping had not been as well-concealed to their neighbors on the mountain as they had thought.

Vincent and Chloe stayed behind, and the four of them sat together on the deck that evening, watching the sun go down. There was a chill in the air as they listened to Vincent relate how easily his story regarding Tony's demise had been accepted by his minions. He reached out and took Chloe's hand when he had finished.

Kendra noticed this and was happy for them.

"To tell you the truth, I think just about the whole organization breathed a sigh of relief," Vincent added.

"He was an evil man," she said.

"Not only evil but crazy," Vincent agreed.

Kendra rose, leaned down, and kissed him on the cheek. "Thank you, Vincent," she said, her voice low, "thank you for killing him."

Garth regarded her, thinking there was an iron side to his wife, wondering if she was aware of its presence.

Kendra settled in Garth's lap and kissed him on the lips.

Both were getting a little antsy now, wanting to be by themselves.

Vincent grinned, picking up on this. "We better get going. It's a long drive back."

While Kendra hugged Chloe, Garth shook with Vincent and thanked him, thinking, If my police brothers could see this, they'd think I was nuts.

Kendra walked Vincent to his car, her arm through his, leaning against him. "So, are you head honcho now?"

He smiled at her. "Nah. What I was hoping would happen did. Everybody just kind of scattered to the wind. I'm what you might say unemployed at the moment."

Chloe took Vincent's other arm. "We're thinking about moving to the Bahamas, buying a fishing boat, living a simple life."

Garth joined them and Kendra stepped away, put her arms around his waist, and rested her head against his shoulder. "I know you'll be very happy, whatever you do together. God be with you and protect you, Vincent."

Vincent seemed startled by that but recovered quickly. He reached out and chucked her under the chin, saying, "Take care of yourself, kid," the same thing he used to say to his baby sister, then was gone.

"We'll probably never see him again," Kendra said.

Garth nodded. "That's the way it should be, Keni."

They gazed at one another for a long moment.

"Let's go inside," he said.

She smiled.

And later, after their marriage had been consummated, after their love had been sated, she rested on top of him, placed her hands on each side of his head, brought her face close to his, and looked into his eyes. Grazing his lips with her own, she whispered against his mouth, "There's something I've been meaning to tell you." Her lips then traveled to his ear where her teeth pulled at the lobe, then tenderly kissed there. She raised up, looked him in the eyes, and, a glow in her own, said, "I'm pregnant." She smiled at his response.

The End

Christy Tillery French

0-595-29123-6

Printed in the United States
25224LVS00003B/232-234